MY NAME IS

Phillis Wheatley

A STORY OF SLAVERY AND FREEDOM

MY NAME IS

Phillis Wheatley

A STORY OF

Slavery

AND

Freedom

Afua Cooper

KCP FICTION
An Imprint of Kids Can Press

To my two daughters, Lamarana and Habiba, who served as muse
during the writing of this book.

KCP Fiction is an imprint of Kids Can Press

Text © 2009 Afua Cooper

Kids Can Press acknowledges the financial support of the Government of Ontario,
through the Ontario Media Development Corporation's Ontario Book Initiative;
the Ontario Arts Council; the Canada Council for the Arts; and the Government
of Canada, through the BPIDP, for our publishing activity.

Published in Canada by   Published in the U.S. by
Kids Can Press Ltd.   Kids Can Press Ltd.
29 Birch Avenue   2250 Military Road
Toronto, ON M4V 1E2   Tonawanda, NY 14150

www.kidscanpress.com

Edited by Charis Wahl
Designed by Marie Bartholomew
Printed and bound in Canada

This book is printed on acid-free paper that is 100% ancient-forest friendly
(100% post-consumer recycled).

CM 09 0 9 8 7 6 5 4 3 2 1

Library and Archives Canada Cataloguing in Publication

Cooper, Afua
        My name is Phillis Wheatley : a story of slavery and
freedom / written by Afua Cooper.

ISBN 978-1-55337-812-9

1. Wheatley, Phillis, 1753–1784—Juvenile fiction. 2. Poets,
American—Colonial period, ca. 1600-1775—Biography—Juvenile
fiction. 3. Slaves—United States—Biography—Juvenile fiction.
4. African American poets—Biography—Juvenile fiction. I. Title.

PS8555.O584M93 2009   jC813'.54   C2008-907592-7

An Hymn to the Morning

Attend my lays, ye ever honour'd nine,

Assist my labours, and my strains refine;

In smoothest numbers pour the notes along,

For bright Aurora now demands my song.

Prologue

MY NAME IS PHILLIS WHEATLEY. I WAS BORN FREE. I WAS MADE A SLAVE. NOW I AM FREE AGAIN. I WAS BORN IN SENEGAL, WEST AFRICA. ONE DAY, SLAVE-TRADERS RAIDED MY TOWN AND KILLED OR CAPTURED US. THEY SOLD ME AND HUNDREDS OF OTHERS TO A SLAVER FROM BOSTON, NEW ENGLAND.

In Boston, Mr. and Mrs. Wheatley bought me to be Mrs. Wheatley's personal slave. They used me well. I learned to speak, read and write the English language. I soon began writing poems, and my mistress had them published in newspapers. Everyone called me a prodigy, the African genius, Boston's brilliant poet. Then I travelled to England as the guest of the Countess of Huntingdon, who published a book of my poetry.

I am writing this autobiographical account so that others will come to know of my extraordinary journey from freedom to slavery and to freedom again. Many will claim they know Phillis Wheatley, but only I can relate the authentic narrative of my past life. But where shall I begin? With my despair or with my triumph? Do I start with my life as an African child? Or my sufferings on the slave ship? Shall I begin with describing the first time I wrote a complete poem and tell of the sweet joy that flowed through my body?

No. I shall begin with what I see shimmering in front of me: Lady Huntingdon's grand reception room in London, England. I am transported on the wings of Aurora, the goddess of the dawn. The date is 30 June, the year 1773. I am nineteen years old.

CHAPTER ONE

Beginnings

The green silk gown does me well, likewise the white bonnet. My mistress had insisted that I dress plainly. Strands of my undisciplined locks peek from my bonnet. I pinch myself. This cannot be happening to me. To *me*. Phillis Wheatley.

There is a knock on my door. "Miss Wheatley, it's time to go down." Amelia, the Irish woman assigned as my maid, stands on the landing. "You look beautiful, ma'am."

"Thanks, Amelia."

As I begin my walk down the stairs, I hear a cheer. The smooth leather of my shoes rests comfortably against my ankles. Good, soft Moroccan leather. But not really Moroccan. Nathaniel, my young master, told me that the leather is actually from Hausaland in West Africa. Hausa traders cross the Sahara Desert and sell the leather to the Moroccans. From Morocco the leather is exported to Europe, so Europeans named it after that country. Nonetheless, it is from Africa, just like me. And it gladdens my heart that I have a bit of Africa with me as I descend the final stair and enter the expectant throng. They cheer.

I have the manuscript in my hand. Thirty-nine poems. *My* book. I glance at the pages and then raise my eyes. Lady Selina Hastings, Countess of Huntingdon, smiles serenely at me. I quickly look around the room. There is the Earl of Dartmouth and his Lady; the Countess of Chatham; Lady Cavendish; the very wealthy businessman Brook Watson; John Thornton, the philanthropist who has given his entire wealth to missionary causes; Lord and Lady Lincoln; and Lady Jane Grey and her daughter Emma. The upper crust of British society. Among them are writers and publishers of the leading London newspapers. And I, an African girl of nineteen years, here to read my poetry to them so that they will buy many copies of my book and encourage their friends and family to patronize me.

My mistress, Susanna Wheatley, has sent me to London to oversee the publication of my poems. I could not find a willing publisher in Boston. Doors were closed to me there, but a great one has opened in London. Lady Huntingdon, a friend of my mistress, agreed to cover some of the costs. My mistress will pay the rest.

I select two pages from the manuscript, but the words swim in front of my eyes. I see flashes of light on the surface of a broad river. A little child pushes aside some bulrushes, and I am swimming in a clear blue pool with my mother. With the sharpness of the morning sun piercing the fog, more scenes unfold: children running behind cattle on a dusty track, women with gourds on their heads going to the well for water, old people sitting under the great baobab tree chewing kola nuts and talking about the latest news. My thoughts flee London to a dusty Senegalese savanna.

I am with little brother, Chierno, and my friends Fanta, Abbi and Mumbi. We hide behind an overgrown baobab tree. I push my head around the trunk and see my elder brother, Amadi, coming along the path with his herd. I signal my playmates to keep still. The cattle pass, their hooves drumming a steady rhythm on the solid dirt. As soon as the last one goes by, we run behind them and let loose small pebbles from our hands. Startled, the cows move faster, plodding into one another, and laughter erupts from our bellies. Amadi, noticing the commotion, turns and we run in the opposite direction.

"Penda, I will get you for this," he yells. "And the rest of you, I will tell your mothers." But we stick out our tongues at him and double over with laughter.

Now I am in my house, engaged in music lessons with my mother. Her name is Asta. She is a griot, a bard, a praise singer and poet, and it is understood that I will follow her path. My mother's mother and her mother before her were griots. It is my family's calling. We memorize our people's history, laws, customs and traditions, and recite these narratives as poetry, admonitions, lectures and songs. Our family carried the traditions of our people even as they moved across great tracts of land in their many migrations. First they were in Macina, in Mali. Then they moved to Fouta Djallon, in Guinea. Numerous clans crossed the mountains and descended onto the plains of the Gambia. Some settled there, but others moved up the wide savannas of Senegal until they arrived at the edge of the desert in Fouta Toro. Several families pushed on, as if seeking the edge of the world. And they did not stop until they reached Mauretania.

Our clans have such names as Wane, Diallo, Ba, Sow, Sidibe, Barri, Watt, Tall, Maal. My clan name is Wane.

My family clan and several others settled here in the kingdom of Fouta Toro on the banks of the Senegal River. My mother used to sing and recite poetry at royal events, at births, marriages, deaths, initiation ceremonies, at happy events and sad ones, too. She and my father would travel great distances, for her fame as a griot spread. She even journeyed as far as Timbuktu and Djenne to sing at the coronations of kings. Because I was to follow in the footsteps of my mother, my formal training began when I was about three years old. By seven, I had achieved some competence (by my mother's high standards), and my mother felt I was good enough to perform at some celebrations in our town, such as the return of the initiated girls from their seclusion, when the entire town made a large celebration for them. I was among the praise singers who welcomed them back and to their new womanhood.

I see my little self being coached by my mother.

She plays on a small guitar that we call an oud. I sing melodies. "Open your mouth this way," she gently coaxes, while showing me the gesture. "Lift the sound up from your belly." And I try. "Good, good." At this age, I know an entire repertoire of praise poems that includes our ancestors' journey from the highlands of Guinea.

Now I am with Ma Ndiaye. When I turned six, my mother sent me to her to train in the composition of sung poems. Our people have diverse ways of composing poetry. Mastering at least eight methods means that one is accomplished. Ma Ndiaye is a formidable reciter and praise singer. She is teaching me a rhyming pattern. Every second line is rhymed, and each line must have eight syllables. Ma Ndiaye sighs heavily. I am getting mixed up. Ma Ndiaye says wearily, "See you tomorrow and remember to practice." I promise myself that I will practice and practice until I grasp the rhyming pattern. I dream of the day when, like my mother, I can sing at royal courts.

Now I see my father in his workshop. He is a weaver. He is named Chierno, like my little brother. Whenever I think of him, I remember him feeding us sweetmeats and yogurt. How he indulged us.

My mother would scold him not to give us snacks before a meal, but he always did. In our country, women spin cotton and dye the thread, but it is the men who weave it. My father's workshop sits to the side of our mud-brick home. He has three apprentices, who set the shuttle and lay out the strips of cotton. My father knows how to weave stories into patterns. Stories of battles, wars, celebrations, journeys and migrations. He is training my little brother to follow in his footsteps.

In our household there are my mother and father; me, Penda; my young brother, Chierno; my older brother, Amadi, the cowherd; and the baby — the apple of our eye and our greatest joy. The baby is a mere nine months old, but my mother says she has the wisdom of a ninety-year-old. Her name is Asta, like my mother.

Our town, Tumbakulli, sits on the banks of the Senegal River. It is protected by a circular wooden wall. At the center is our chief's house and the mosque. We are a settlement of weavers, herders, farmers, griots and fishermen.

"Alif, Ba, Taa. Tha ..." The sound of children's voices, one of them my own, echoes in my head. We are at school, sitting on the floor on straw mats, in a semicircle. In front of us is our teacher, Baba Dende, and we are practicing our letters. Our school, a long rectangular building built of mud bricks, sits beside the house of our teacher. Boys and girls arrive at school in the evening, when the sun loses some of its power and a coolness descends on the earth. Sometimes it is still hot, though, and Baba Dende gives us our lessons beneath the great baobab in the center of the town. We learn the Arabic alphabet so we can read and recite verses from our holy book, the Qur'an. My brother Chierno is very accomplished. He knows at least a quarter of the holy book by heart, and sometimes he acts as Baba Dende's helper.

In the evening, our voices resound across the village and beyond, as we shout the alphabet in a loud and rhythmic chant. And we think of the beginning of the dry season, when holy men and women wander through the countryside singing religious songs.

Once, when I was about six years old, a group of these holy singers arrived from Macina, in the old kingdom of Mali. There was a woman among them, as tall and straight as a tree. She wore a billowing dress we call a boubou; the dress was green and her head was wrapped with a cloudy-white turban. She sang in a high-pitched voice that seemed to shoot straight into the sky, descend to earth and vibrate across the desert. She had a funny accent, as do all the Fulani from Mali, but her singing was so beautiful, so melodious that the adults began to cry, and tears also rolled down my face. This woman had a great reputation. It was said that when family members were estranged from each other, they would call on her to heal their troubles with her singing. Her songs were about how to live a righteous life, songs about this world and the next.

Days after the singing woman left our town, I would try to sing like her — pitching my voice to the sky and commanding it to bounce to the earth. But both my mother and Ma Ndiaye laughed out loud and shouted at me to stop. "Not now, Penda, not now. Wait a few more years, when your voice is mature."

The sky is a clear blue and the sun a golden orb. The heat presses on us from all sides. The baby is fussy. The voice of the muezzin weaves through the heat. After prayers, my mother gathers the baby and me and we head toward the river, to the section where the women swim and bathe with the small children. The pool is surrounded by bulrushes, some of which hang over the water forming a natural roof, sheltering us from the unforgiving sun. And the water is shallow. I could go to the center and the water would only reach my shoulders. Smaller children hug the bank. We swim and frolic, and snack on the sweets our mothers have brought. After the river bath, we head home. I run to my father in his workshop, and he lifts me up to his shoulders and tosses me in the air like a ball of cotton. I shriek with delight. Even though my father is not a griot, he knows many poems and songs and sings to us. When I am amazed at his knowledge, he says, "All our people are poets."

And it is true. In our country, people do not speak in direct language. For example, if one of us misbehaved in class, Baba Dende would go to the house of the offender. The parents would invite him in and offer tea. After a few sips of tea, they would talk about the weather, the crops, the incoming and outgoing tide of the river, the initiation ceremonies for the boys and girls. Then, after a long while, Baba Dende would broach the subject that was on his mind.

He would say, "Little hyenas are running wild in the town." And the parents would nod their heads mournfully. The conversation would continue in parables and riddles until one of the parents, usually the father, would say, "Baba, I will take the child in hand."

***

A slight touch on my shoulder brings me back to the present. The hand belongs to the Countess of Huntingdon. "Phillis, you ought to eat something." In truth, I cannot. I am not nervous. I prepared for this evening all day. But my stomach seems full.

Without another word, the countess takes the manuscript from my hand and summons a servant. He brings a tray heaped with cake slices and buns. I take a bun. Another servant brings drinks. I avoid the wine but select an orange punch.

The Earl of Dartmouth comes to where the countess and I stand.

"What will our young African genius read for us tonight?"

"Don't be impatient," the countess rebukes him. "You will soon know well." And to me she says, "Sit, Phillis. Sit and eat."

I collapse into a satin-cushioned chair. How soft it is. I eat the bun in small bites. I gulp the punch. I am excited. After what seems like an eternity, the countess calls the room to order and speaks:

"As you know, we are gathered here tonight to hear young Phillis Wheatley, the African genius from Boston. We call Phillis a genius because she is only nineteen years old and already has written many poems and has had them published in newspapers. The printing of Phillis's book is sponsored by my organization. We expect the book to be ready for sale in September. Phillis and her poetry are wonderful examples of the workings of God. He has lifted a lowly, benighted African girl and has given her the gift of words and rhyme."

A thundering applause greets the countess's words. "Now Phillis will read for us."

A space has been cleared in the middle of the living room beside the fortepiano. A lamp burns brightly. The light will be good for my reading. I walk to the appointed space. I survey the crowd. Most came out of curiosity. To see if a Black girl could really write and read poetry. To see if a Black girl had literary talent. Others do not believe that I have written the verses.

A hush descends. In my mind, I hear Mrs. Wheatley, my mistress: "Look at them with confidence, hold that confidence in your voice." I hear my young Master John's voice: "Stand firm, Phillis, and let your heart say the words." And the voice of my mother, my mother whom I have not seen in eleven years: "Penda, recite with feelings and passion. Let the words and verses come alive."

Sweet memories now make my heart ache with longing and sorrow. I decide to begin with "On Recollection," the poem that invokes Mneme, the Greek goddess of memory, inventor of words and language and mother of the nine Muses. I inhale and then exhale the poem:

Mneme begin. Inspire, ye sacred nine,
Your vent'rous Afric in her great design.
Mneme, immortal pow'r, I trace thy spring:
Assist my strains, while I thy glories sing:

As I read, the power of words fills me with confidence and strength. The poem is met with thunderous applause.

21

I decide that the next poem should be the one I wrote for Lord Dartmouth. Because he is here at Lady Huntingdon's and because he has been so good to me since I arrived—he has given me five pounds and the complete collection of Milton's works—I read "To the Right Honourable William, Earl of Dartmouth."

The Earl of Dartmouth has been appointed secretary of the American colonies. The Americans hope that he will listen to their complaints and do right by them. They are being taxed by the British on almost everything but do not have representation in the British Parliament. Now they are almost up in arms, demanding their freedom from British "slavery."

Hail, happy day, when, smiling like the morn,
Fair Freedom *rose* New-England *to adorn:*
The northern clime beneath her genial ray,
Dartmouth, *congratulates thy blissful sway:*
Elate with hope her race no longer mourns…
No more America, in mournful strain
Of wrongs, and grievance unredress'd complain,
No longer shalt thou dread the iron chain,
Which wanton Tyranny *with lawless hand*

Had made, and with it meant t'enslave the land...
I, young in life, by seeming cruel fate
Was snatch'd from Afric's fancy'd happy seat...
Such, such my case. And can I then but pray
Others may never feel tyrannic sway?

The Earl of Dartmouth looks at me, bows from his waist and leads the applause. I bask in the praise and recognition Lady Huntingdon and her friends bestow on me. "Is this me?" "Did I just do what I did?" "Am I the girl that everyone now loves?" And I answer all three questions: "Yes!"

***

Two days later, Amelia brings me the newspapers. I smile when I see the headlines: "Phillis Wheatley, American African Poet Conquers London." "The Ethiopian Poetess and Her Surprising Genius." They are flattering articles. The *Monthly Review* states that I should be given my freedom, that I am much too talented to be kept in bondage. The writer says that Bostonians pride themselves on the principles of liberty, yet they hold one such as I in slavery. "Oh ye America, give Phillis her freedom!" the *Review* proclaims.

Another newspaper calls me the "mother of Black literature." It seems I am the first African woman in this part of the world to have a book published. I shake my head in wonderment at this praise. Of course I am flattered, but I quickly remember my mistress telling me not to get too big a head from the acclaim that would be heaped on me.

That evening, my publisher, Archibald Bell, visits the house. He takes off his hat and bows to me. He kisses Lady Huntingdon's hand. "Ladies, I have good news. Phillis, the manuscript is gone to press!" he says. The countess claps her hands. I simply stare. Since neither of us speaks, Mr. Bell continues. "There are already three hundred subscribers!" This must mean that sufficient buyers have agreed to purchase copies to make printing profitable for him. Finally, Lady Huntingdon says, "Well done, Phillis. God is on our side."

Though I prepare for sleep, the excitement of the past days courses through my mind and body, and I am unable to relax. I am happy, of course, but the words from the newspapers rush around in my head: "Phillis Wheatley, a slave." "Genius in bondage." Though used well, I am a slave, it is true. But it was not always so.

CHAPTER TWO

Capture

Through the dust storm, beyond the wall of the town, we saw the cowherds with their cattle. My friends and I wanted to pelt the cows, but they were too fast for us. Instead, we watched. No sooner did the herds thunder by than we saw a lone rider coming from the horizon. His horse ran with such haste. From the center of the village, we heard the sound of the cow horn alerting the people. My friends and I ran to the gate of the town. Uthman Tall, a friend of my father, opened the gate. Horse and rider thundered through. In an instant, a crowd gathers at the square. The rider dismounts. He walks briskly to the chief. They greet each other in formal language. Then Chief Ibrahima says, "Speak to us. I know you bring news of great urgency."

The man spoke. "Slave traders are about. *Toubabs*, White men. Seal the gates of your town at dusk. Keep a watch night and day. Go beyond the wall only in groups. Do not allow the children to wander off by themselves. Go about your business carrying your weapons. This is a message from the king."

And with those words the rider changed our lives. Soon the drums were pounding out the message that would travel from village to village, town to town, throughout the whole kingdom. I listened to the rhythmic patterns of the music — "slave-traders," "toubabs," "go about in groups." And I trembled.

My father had seen the toubabs before. He said their skin is as pale as a ghost's. They have stringy hair and big noses. They have almost no lips, and their eyes are of different colors. Even so, my father said, they are human. He saw them when he worked as an apprentice in Djenne. Those toubabs had come to Senegal to trade, but many others wanted to buy people to be slaves in their countries far across the sea.

My mother had also seen a toubab. He had come to Tumbakulli before I was born. My mother said that this man was on his way to discover where the great river Niger ends. The Niger is the river of the world, my mother said. Its source is in the land of our ancestors, the land of Guinea. The Niger winds its way through the empire of Mali. The great cities of Djenne, Timbuktu and Gao sit on its banks. The toubab, my mother said, was from a White country called Scotland. The women of our town touched his skin and told him he ought to sit more in the sun to acquire the complexion of our people. They wondered if his nose was real. It was big and pointy. And they asked him why he would leave his family to find out where the Niger ends.

This man stayed for two weeks on his way to Timbuktu. Oftentimes, you would hear people say, "It was at least fifteen rainy seasons before the toubab came to Tumbakulli" or "It was after the toubab passed through our village."

But most toubabs did not seek the sources and destinations of rivers. Many came to buy the bodies of Africans. My father had said he had seen White men called French in their fort at Saint-Louis with groups of captured Africans huddled together, forlorn, terrified and weary. They were sent to the land of the toubabs, and no one knew what happened to them. They were never seen again. I listened to my father, and I was afraid.

After the messenger rode away, the chief raised his hands, but there was no need to because everyone was as still as stones. "You have heard the messenger, and you will abide by what he says. We will now organize the watch and strengthen our fortifications." I thought of my brother and the other cowherds outside the walls. As if reading my mind, the chief said, "The cowherds will have heard the message of the drums. Nonetheless, I will send someone to warn them."

Our lives changed with the coming of the messenger. At first, my friends and I still played games outside the gates, but we stayed close to the wall under the watchful eye of the guards. After a few days, we were not permitted to play outside the walls. When the women and children went to swim and bathe and carry water from the pools of the Senegal, they were accompanied by guards. My brother and his fellow cowherds carried spears and bows and arrows while herding their cattle. Older men carried the guns they acquired in trade with the Moors, Mandinka or toubabs.

The fear remained constant and was often punctuated by news that a village had been attacked by slavetraders and the people carried off. Yet trade caravans still came. The men with their faces covered with blue veils. They rode on camels, sometimes with wives and children. Moors and Tuareg. From Mauretania and Morocco and even from Algeria. Mandinka caravans on their way to and from the highlands of Guinea, from the Gambia, from Mali. Hausa traders from such distant places as Sokoto, Zaria and Bornu in the east. They traded cloth, rice, millet, corn and sorghum. Dried fish, alligator skin, elephant tusk, amber, gold, cloves, peppers and other spices.

We were having supper when we heard the commotion. The crying of the animals, the shouts and screams of the villagers: "Slave raiders, slave raiders!"

Father grabbed baby Asta, who was sleeping on a cot beside mother. "Come!" he yelled.

My mother hesitated and reached into a wicker basket for food for the baby.

"Asta!" my father shrieked. He held the baby to his chest with one hand, and with the other held my hand. We bolted from the house just in time. We heard a loud explosion and saw bright flames fill the air. An acrid smell assaulted my nostrils. I turned and see my mother fall. That was the last I see of her.

More booming explosions and the burning smell. I felt my lungs tightening and heard the furious drum of my heart. There was a pounding in my head. I held tightly to my father's hand, and we got through the gates of the town and stumble through thick undergrowth. What of my mother? I pushed the thought from my mind. I must not think, but run, run, run. We staggered through the dark night with our townspeople. We reached a hilltop, and my father stopped to look back. A furious blaze brightened the night. The town was on fire.

The baby began to wail, and I whispered, "Papa, my legs are tired, I cannot go on." My poor father starts to say something, but shadows emerged from the thicket and throw him to the ground. I screamed, but not for long, because rough and powerful hands covered my mouth and I fell. A blow to my head and I sank into a thick blackness.

When I came to, dawn was peeping through the darkness. I felt a pressure on my wrists. They were tied together with a length of thick rope. I was certain that my mother and many other villagers had been killed in the attack. What had become of my father and baby sister I did not know. What has happened to my elder brother, Amadi, I had no idea. When the slave raiders arrived he was with his cattle in the grazing lands beyond the town. My little brother, Chierno, was at our uncle's house. Did he survive?

In an instant, my life had changed. One moment I was basking in the warm embrace of my family. The next, I was dragged away, shackled to a slave coffle — a group of captives. Slave raiders had reaped a bountiful harvest. There were women with babies on their backs and at their bosoms. Young children like me, teenagers, grandparents and people my parents' age. Some had been captured from neighboring villages on the banks of the Senegal. We began a trek to the mouth of the Gambia River, which flows into the Atlantic Ocean. It is a journey of several hundred kilometers. We walked. I was eight years old.

CHAPTER THREE

Vultures

We walked under the hot sun, the vultures flying low overhead. Along with the sun, a fever burned my body. Sharp images of my mother and the baby danced before my eyes. I cried out. But to no avail. The more I cried, the farther away they became. I stumbled, but the weight of the coffle held me up. Every limb of my body ached. My feet felt like hot iron. I knew I would die, as surely as Yasin Balde, the cowherd who was attacked by a hungry lioness. Finally, the owner of the coffle put me in a basket carried by two other captives. This was a mercy because I had some protection from the sun. For days I remained unconscious. In these spells I was with my parents, my baby sister and brothers, and we were swimming and bathing in the pool and eating sweetmeats. Other times, I was with my friends, throwing stones after my brother's cattle or mimicking and frustrating our poor teacher, Baba Dende.

Sometimes cool drops from the sudden rains brought me to consciousness. During such times, I forced myself to fall asleep again. I refused to face what was happening around me. When babies died, they were snatched from their screaming mothers and thrown into the bush. The buzzards that accompanied us had their reward. The hot sun, the endless walking and the starvation also claimed some of the adults, especially the grandparents. There would be a jerking motion in the coffle and we would pitch forward. A guard immediately freed the dead from their chains and threw the bodies into the bush. Every day someone died. Every day the vultures, messengers of death, accompanied us, and when they sensed that someone was about to die, they circled around our heads.

After many days, the intense heat disappeared and it became cooler. I sat up and saw a landscape of green, trees tall and thick and covered with broad leaves. We were passing through a true forest. We waded across small streams. Rainbow-colored birds arched toward the sky, and their sounds resounded through the air. Soon we came to a small town. We first approached the fields. Rows and rows of corn and twines of peas. We passed an area of dense cotton cultivation. Men and small children stood guard with tall sticks and stones to chase away monkeys. As our coffle approached, the townspeople talked excitedly and pointed to us. They spoke Mandinka, which I understood, though I could not speak it. We pressed on and came to a swampy area. Women stood knee-deep in the water. Slim shoots protruded from the mud. Rice. Rice. Rice. The women looked mournfully at us. In spite of my condition, I was struck by the beauty of the place. Every plant seemed to be in bloom. The hills and dales were round and green. Streams made the place cool and fertile. Even the blue of the sky was soft on the eye. The inhabitants appeared healthy. The coffle moved on.

The air grew even cooler, and I felt my lungs opening. I lay back in my basket, my head swimming from all that I had seen. But excited chatter made me rise again and look in wonder. Before us spread a broad river. It seemed to go on forever. It was the River Gambia. And it led to the sea. The excited murmurs from the coffle turned into wails, and even I, feeling as if I had only one breath left, joined in the mournful song.

The Atlantic opened out in front of us like a wide scarf, the color of the sky. The foamy waves rushed to the shore and then back into the arms of the wide ocean. My father had seen the ocean and had told me about it. And I had wished one day to see it. But not like this. Not like this. A thousand smells sought my nostrils: of fish fresh and stale, the salt of the sea and other scents, foul ones, carried by the wind. The sea birds screeched their stories in deafening tones.

We were lodged in the dungeon of a "slave castle," built by toubabs from a country called Germany. Later, it was captured by the English, who called it Fort James. The English were in command when my coffle arrived. The captives were hoarded in the dungeon until a ship came from Europe or America to buy them. Sometimes, captives waited at Fort James for more than two months. Fortunately, our wait was only one week. I say fortunately because Fort James was a living hell. The dungeon was dark and stank with a hundred vile odors. Chinks of light came from one tiny window. A massive iron door blocked our way. With chains around our feet and hands, we lay in our filth and misery. Some wailed and shrieked, others emitted a low moan. I was too weak and frightened to do either.

Then one day, White men with guns came and opened the iron door. They hustled us up the stairs, our chains making an awful sound, into the blinding light above. A ship had entered the harbor. The captain of the ship did not want to buy me — I would be of no use to any slaveholder, not in America, not in Brazil, not in the Caribbean. But the trader persuaded him, and he bought me for a quarter of the price paid for a child my age.

On that day, more than three hundred captives boarded the ship with me. Some were children, others were advanced in age, but most were young men and women, teenagers and young adults. Canoes took us out to the waiting ship. Even though I was feverish, the sight of the ship was alarming. It was like a monstrous wooden bird, with wings white and broad. The ship bounced up and down on the water. As the canoes drew near to the ship, I made out bold letters on its side: P-H-I-L-L-I-S. I knew that meant something, but what I did not know. I had studied my letters with Baba Dende, but they did not look like this. These letters were straight and angular. The letters I had learned in my village school were soft and curvy. The letters on the side of the ship danced into my head until, once again, I blacked out.

But fainting could not save me. We were herded onto the ship like chained cattle. A mournful cry went up, the children crying for their mothers. "Mama, Maaa, Umi, Amma." Some tried to jump overboard but were held back by the toubab sailors. The adults wept, too, howls bursting from the depths of their bowels. Some silently stared into space. A fearsome noise beat against my brain, and my body convulsed as I lay on the wooden planks, wet with water, wet with fear.

The men were shackled two by two. The right wrist and ankle of one were attached by chains to the left wrist and ankle of another. And so, cross-shackled, they shuffled along the deck. Toubab men with guns pointed the men to a stairway down into the ship. The women and children sat on the open deck, though the women who were heavy with child were sent into a makeshift room on the deck. Mercifully, neither the women nor the children were chained. Did the toubabs not think we were dangerous? Did they believe they could control women and children more easily than men? Is that why our fathers and brothers were shackled like beasts?

How long I lay on the cold planks I do not know. Amid the noise, I slept, my body broken by exhaustion. And, as I slept, my spirit flew back to Fouta Toro. All around me I saw the smoldering ruin of my town. Dead and dying cattle sprawled in the corral. Rotting bodies of humans. I searched for my mother and sister but did not find them. I willed myself to escape from the dream. I entered another dream. My family and I were sitting in the town square and watching a camel caravan enter the town. Fifty camels! What a sight. Merchants had come to trade. They were going to the land of Mali. My father was feeding me sour cream mixed with honey.

"It is a dream. That is all, my child."

I opened my eyes to see a woman bent over me. She had a green shawl over her shoulders. I gazed at the woman and tried to figure out who she was and where I was. But a sound was coming from somewhere. A low moan. "It's only a dream, my child," the woman said in my language. The sound was coming from me. And I remembered the dream. I had woken up crying. My face was wet with my tears. I turned away from the woman, moaning louder, the taste of honey and sour cream still in my mouth.

She touched me softly on my shoulders. Like my own mother.

"Who are you?" I asked.

"Does it matter who anyone of us is? We could be kings and queens, merchants, mothers or daughters. Does it matter?" The woman looked like a noble woman, her face, her bearing, her manner of speech. How did she get that shawl? And how was she wearing a long penne wrapped around her waist when most of us were naked?

The woman propped me up and wiped my face with her shawl. She wrapped her arms around me. For so long I had not known such tenderness. I wept aloud. I would not see my mother again. Would never touch her, feel her breath, inhale her smell of musk, watch as she made porridge or dyed cotton indigo. She would never teach me to sing again. I would never bathe with her in the pool along the banks of the Senegal. As these thoughts raced through my head, I was seized with a fit of trembling that would not cease.

The ship began to move like the earth moving beneath my feet. The others felt it, too. Screams flew back and forth, and from below deck came the loud and mournful sounds of the chained men. Some cried, others prayed. Prayers sent to the God of their fathers, prayers sent to Allah: *Rescue us from the evils of this day.* We were leaving the land of the Gambia, the land of the Senegal, the land of Guinea. We were leaving the lands of our mothers, the countries of our fathers. The verdant landscape became a green line across the horizon. Then Africa disappeared from view, became one with the sky, and my heart changed position in my chest.

Planks were laid out on the deck for small children like me to sleep on. Fulani and Mandinka and Wolof children. There were twin girls, Natta and Néné, a boy named Hassanu and a child around six years old who looked like my brother, Chierno. He was called Jibril. But in my heart I named him Chierno. That night we crowded together. He shivered all the time and kept his eyes closed. My fever came and went.

The blackness was broken occasionally by toubab men walking the deck with lanterns. I looked up to the sky, and the stars twinkled at me. I remembered that when it was very hot at night, the townspeople would gather on the rock outside our town and air themselves. My father would point to the sky and name each star. I would cuddle close to him, and he would embrace me. "And that one," he would say, pointing to Venus, "is you. The brightest star of all."

I felt Jibril trembling beside me. "It will be all right, Jibril, it will be all right." I hugged him and gazed at the sky. The ship plowed through the dark waters to our certain death.

Morning came. It came too soon. Beneath me the ship heaved and rolled. The movement of the boat made me dizzy, and I placed my palm over my heaving stomach to calm it. I kept my eyes closed, though the light from the day penetrated them. There were still the cries and moans. Jibril lay beside me, still as a stone. His trembling had ceased. For that I was grateful. No sooner had the thought entered my mind than I felt a rude poke in my ribs. My eyes flew open. A toubab was prodding me with his hand, hairy as a monkey. Toubabs have a lot of hair on their bodies. He was speaking his funny language.

"*That one looks dead,*" he said, pressing his hand in my side, but pointing to Jibril.

Another toubab was standing over our little group. The twins were also awake and, seeing the toubab standing over us, cried softly. "*Looks like it,*" the other toubab said. "*Let's throw him over.*"

Their gestures and tones caused me to look at Jibril. He lay calmly, his face full of sweetness. I touched his forehead. It was cool. I smiled inwardly. Jibril was at rest. One of the toubabs scooped him up and walked toward the side of the ship. But the woman in the green shawl shouted, "No, wait. Give him to me." And, with one mighty bound, she snatched Jibril out of his hands. On hearing her shout, several toubabs ran toward the woman and pointed their guns. But she ignored them. She laid Jibril on the deck and prayed over him. Then she held him in her arms and kissed his face.

"*Give him to me,*" the toubab yelled. He pushed the woman aside, scooped up Jibril and tossed his body into the sea as if he were a piece of firewood. Had Jibril been home, mourners, mainly women, some close relatives, would have sung their songs of lament and sorrow. They would have rent the air with their wails and told that Jibril was a sweet child, an angel. Then women would have bathed his body in water perfumed with cloves and musk. They would have dried it and anointed it with shea butter, wrapped it in soft white cotton cloth and laid him to rest, before sunset, in the town's cemetery. His people would have kept a vigil and prayed throughout the night of his burial, speeding his soul to paradise with their prayers.

CHAPTER FOUR

Middle Passage

I had a notion that soon I would follow Jibril to paradise. Toubabs with guns herded us on the deck. We were sure they were going to kill us. But soon we heard the clanking of chains and low moans. The men were coming up on deck! Some kept their heads down. They were ashamed. Ashamed that we, their children and wives, their sisters and mothers, would see them in their powerlessness. They were also ashamed to see our shame and powerlessness. Some looked up and around, looked for a long time at the sky. "*Move,*" the toubab yelled. The men moved. As they shuffled forward, they left behind red streaks. I looked at their feet. The men's ankles were a mass of bleeding, pus-filled flesh. A great stench rose in the air. "*Stop, stop now!*" Another order from the toubab. Then some of the sailors attached the iron around each of the men's legs to a great chain that ran along both sides of the ship. I prepared myself for a great slaughter.

But the toubabs were only feeding us breakfast.

We held out our hands as they passed with a huge iron pot and a large wooden spoon. They dumped boiled rice with bits of meat into our hands. I heard a firm voice saying, "Don't eat it." But some of us, consumed by hunger, took the food. I ate slowly, trying to steady myself against the ship's rocking, and I felt that I was going to pass out. But the voice spoke again. "They are feeding us the meat of the pig." My stomach churned and heaved, and in an instant I vomited what I had eaten. My vomit spewed across the toubab and fell right into the iron pot.

"I'll be damned! Get that one away. I'm sure she is ill." Another toubab led me to my plank of wood. The earth was spinning. Then cramping pains contracted my stomach. I held my face between my hands and felt myself sinking and sinking. Wait for me, Jibril! Wait for me!

I was delirious for a long time. I would come into consciousness and find the woman with the green shawl bending over me. Then I remembered where I was, and I willed myself to faint again. Once, when I woke up, fever burned my body, and thick raindrops were falling on me. The water was cool, but the fever held me. I woke again and found myself with other children in the hut built on deck for the pregnant women. Many children were ill. The woman in green was our nurse. I decided that she was one of the angels that Baba Dende had taught us about.

"Eat, child, eat. Eat so you will live. The ancestors and God demand that you live." The woman was pressing cooked millet between my lips, but the stench from the hut assaulted my nostrils and I could not eat. When last had we bathed? The floor of the hut was covered in slime: vomit, mucus and our bodily waste. The angel, as if sensing my thought, said, "The captain said today he will give us vinegar to clean the deck. But now you must eat. Do it for Jibril." At the sound of Jibril's name I let out a deep howl and could not be consoled.

How many nights and days passed before the fever left my body I do not know, but when it finally subsided I had become as thin as a skeleton. I was grateful to be in the hut because I could shield my eyes from the grossest humiliations meted out to our people: "exercise," for the men chained in the bottom of the ship.

The men of my nation were among the tallest people of the region. When I was with my father, he seemed tall as a tree. My brother Amadi, though he was only fourteen, had the height of a grown man, and my mother said he had not yet attained his full stature. But here men lay on platforms in the belly of the ship. The space between platforms was less than three feet. So the men could not even sit up, but had to lie spoon fashion, belly to back, packed tighter than the stacks of pancakes my mother used to make for breakfast. Packed so tightly that no air passed between them. Packed so tightly that they could not turn over. A man in his coffin had more space than these men. And they were chained.

The men could not even rise to answer the call of nature, so they soiled themselves. Their bodily waste, the blood and mucus gave the floor another layer. Every morning, when the sailors went down to hustle the men to breakfast, they would bring up several corpses chained to the living. And the sailors would toss them overboard. There would be no funeral, no wife and children to beat their chests and sing the songs of lamentation. No griot to chant the dirges and tell of the magnificent lives of these men. That that one was a farmer who commanded the largest harvest of rice; that this one was a fisherman to whom the fish surrendered themselves willingly; that another was a hunter who knew the languages of all the animals and the plants of the forest; that yet another was a hafiz, a reciter, who knew the Qur'an by heart. And one was engaged to be married and was snatched from his intended as they stole a moment for themselves on the banks of the Senegal. These were the men tossed to the sharks.

Exercise was supposed to make the men's limbs supple again. The men were ordered to jump up and down. Several toubabs stood with their guns and whips, but how could the men attack them when they were chained?

A captive beat out a rhythm on a broken drum. "*Jump, jump,*" a toubab screeched. He demonstrated jumping up and down on the deck. "*Jump.*" And the men, their chains clanking and the blood flowing from their ankles, jumped awkwardly. And they cried as they did so.

The man who was beating the drum wept and

refused to play. One toubab pointed at him with his gun, while another manacled him.

A toubab played a strange instrument. He blew into a pipe attached to a bag, and a high, sharp sound escaped from the bag. A sailor pointed his gun at the women. "*Now it is your turn. Dance!*" The women formed a ragged circle. "*Dance!*" came the order. And the women sucked the air between their teeth and let out a long hiss. This was an insulting sound, but the toubab did not know this. The women kissed their teeth once more and then rocked their bodies from side to side. "*Sing!*" Another command from a toubab. He opened his mouth and made sounds. We understood. He was asking us to sing. But of what should we sing?

The women sang out in high, clear voices: "May God curse you forever. May your lineage be cut short. May God destroy you and your tribe." This they said as the toubab played the strange instrument. They rocked their bodies from side to side and repeated the curse over and over. Then we sang of our grief and pain, of the loss of our families, our country and our lives. We sang of our terror, and we sang of the guns, the whips, the beatings and clubbings, the deaths, the hunger and the fear. I sang in a whisper, thinking of Jibril, of Chierno, of Amadi, of my parents, of the baby, of my teacher, Baba Dende, of the cows — each one named by Amadi — of the River Senegal, of the River Gambia. I sang of my lost life. We sang in the languages of our mothers and fathers. The words formed around our tongues, in Fullah, in Mandinka, in Serer, in Wolof, even in Hassiniyya, a language of the people of Mauretania. The words slipped from our mouths and spilled our sorrow into the air. And, like the men, we cried as we sang.

After the dancing and singing, the men were led back into the hold of the ship. And were brought up once more for dinner, which was the same as breakfast. After dinner the men were taken back to the ship's dungeon and the gratings closed over them. When the gratings clicked in place, the men would wail, because down below the air was thick and foul and they could hardly breathe. During the night some would die, and the sailors would bring them up in the morning and throw them to the sharks.

All day and all night we pushed through the ocean. Sometimes the sea was the sky, and sometimes the sky was the sea. Sharks followed our ship like the vultures that had accompanied our slave coffle through the savanna and forest, knowing they would be rewarded with human flesh. And how the ship stank! Every week the captain had the toubab sailors scrub the floors of the sleeping rooms with hot vinegar, but it did little to alleviate the stench. As soon as the rooms were cleaned, our sick bodies emitted matter that made the floor slippery again, as if the cleaning had never been done.

Then one day, after we had been at sea for about three weeks, a storm broke. It was after dinner, and the men were at their "exercise." All day the sky had been gray, with a sharp wind, and getting darker. All of a sudden, the sky was filled with rain clouds and the wind picked up speed. Pebbles of rain splattered on the deck. The captain ordered the captive men back into their dungeons. We, the women and children, ran to our makeshift shelters. The captain sent the pregnant women, with guards, to his own cabin. Sheets of red, blue and gold sliced the air, and for a moment hung suspended. The children shrieked. The women whispered words of comfort, but even they seemed afraid. One kept saying that she had never seen lightning the color of gold before. "It must be a sign, and not a good one," she said.

The lightning seemed to last for hours. But this was only the beginning. The rain was pouring from the sky. The wind picked up speed and howled. The ship heaved as if wanting to spew up its wretched cargo. Then the thunder began. First, we heard the low rumble somewhere on the horizon. Then the sound of a thousand drums, low and menacing.

We huddled together, fear gripping our lungs so tightly that we could not breathe. I had been in a thunderstorm in Fouta, but it was not as strong as this one, and I had had my mother's skirt to hide behind, her soothing voice to banish my fears and my father's arms to hold and comfort me. But not here. The rumbling of the thunder crescendoed into a great crash. The sound shot through me and I fell backward. The wind grew even fiercer, and I felt the ship tossing back and forth, back and forth, like a leaf.

Soon water began spilling over the deck, and in no time it came up to our knees. The wind grabbed the canvas that had been our roof and blew it into the sea. The rain hit me with such force that my skin burned as if touched by live coals. The gale picked me up and pushed me toward the side of the ship. I screamed with every bit of energy I had. A toubab sheltering beneath a dripping canvas ran toward me. A woman did the same. Luckily, I caught the chain of iron that the captive men were chained to when they came up for exercise. The woman crawled through the water and grabbed me. The ship tossed back and forth and the wind tried to throw us overboard, but the woman clung to me and I to the iron. Huddled together, we surrendered ourselves to the fury of the storm.

As the woman and I held on against the wind, we heard a low moaning that did not belong to the storm. It was neither wind nor rain, lightning nor thunder. It was the voices of humans, the captive men chained below in the belly of the ship. The portholes had been covered, cutting off fresh air to the hold. The men were suffocating because whatever air remained became thick and stank with a thousand foul smells. Shackled and packed so tightly together, the men gasped for air in the boiling heat of the room. Unable to breathe and with sweat pouring from their bodies, the men began to wail as death took them. Despite the rain, wind, thunder, the fearsome crashes, the sound found its way to us on the deck. "We are dying, we are dying." And the sound filled me with dread and sorrow. "We are dying, we are dying, we are dying." During the night some would die, and the sailors would bring them up in the morning, if morning ever came, and throw them to the sharks.

CHAPTER FIVE

Dirge

The ship did not sink to the bottom of the ocean. The storm ended as abruptly as it began. The winds calmed and became a gentle breeze. The thunder ceased. The lightning halted its fearsome display. And, in an instant, the gray of the sky changed to blue and the sun came out. Now we knew that we were in the hands of some malevolent force. Nature was not so fickle.

The captain passed buckets to the women, and they helped the sailors bail water that had cleaned the deck of its filth. The captain ordered sailors to rebuild the huts for the women and children. We huddled together, tired, weak and afraid. We were also hungry. And the men shackled together below the deck? How many had died?

A melancholy began among us children. We stared into space and refused to eat. The women who became our mothers told us the usual thing, that God and the ancestors wanted us to live. But our ears were beyond their words. Grief had built a wall around us. Our melancholy spread to some of the men and the women. The captain ran around with his *speculum oris* (I later learned the term in my Latin studies with Nathaniel), a mouth opener, to force gruel down our throats. Maybe it was because I was so weak that my lips opened and the captain poured a bad-tasting porridge down my throat. As soon as it hit my stomach, I heaved it up.

But not even the *speculum oris* could pry open the mouths of the twins. They sat, holding hands, their teeth clamped together. The captain made the mistake of prying in their mouths with his finger. He let out a bloodcurling sound when his finger went between Néné's teeth. She bit down and would not stop. When the captain finally extricated his finger, the top of it was missing. Néné spat it out and continued staring into space.

"*You stupid nigger.*" A whip hissed in the air and landed on Néné's back. I turned my head away, ready for her howl. But none came. The twins had passed away from this world.

The next day, madness took over. Three women ran around the deck, shrieking. A sailor cut them down with his gun. The drummer was once again ordered to play. But who could play, dance or sing after witnessing the murder of the women? So the drummer man cursed the toubabs instead. Beasts, murderers, violators of women, devils from hell, savages, satan's angels, he called them. And he jumped up and down, harsh sounds coming from his throat. Then he laughed uncontrollably. Two toubabs ran toward him, held him down and chained him. Then the captain applied the whip. The man's back soon became a mass of raw bleeding flesh, but the captain did not stop. He flogged him until he died.

All day and all night I heard the moans and cries of the men below deck. And the dirges of the women on deck. "What is to become of us? What is to become of us?" we asked in sad tones. Many said that the toubabs were taking us to their country to eat us, but a woman said that the toubabs had big farms, and they would take us there to work night and day. It was a toubab who told her. He had been to Africa many times and knew some of the Mandinka language.

Later, in Massachusetts, I was told that the *Phillis* was a lucky ship: the smallpox and dysentery did not travel with us. When those diseases break out on a slave ship, sometimes half or more of the captives die. But I don't know if we were lucky. So what if the smallpox had broken out on our ship? So what if we had died? It would have been no matter. We had already suffered the dreaded pains of hell.

Days might have passed, but I am not sure. It could have been just one day. However, I heard the excited chatter of the sailors. "*Land, land, we see land!*" They pointed in a certain direction. The women got excited, too. We were coming close to the land of the toubabs. The women's chatter turned into sorrow, and once again they began to sing. They knew that once in the toubab land their lives would continue in misery. I could only wonder if I would get there. I prayed that I would not.

CHAPTER SIX

Boston Slavery

The men were taken up on board and washed down. The floors were swept and cleaned. The women and children were also washed and oiled. They did not bother to clean and oil me and the others who were ill in mind or body. They simply let us lie in our misery. We sailed into Boston Harbor, the land of the toubabs. What strange sights — long wooden houses stacked together, shops, stores and three-story warehouses. And the clamor, the noise of toubab men and women swarming along the dock, pointing at the ship. I heard the strange sounds of their speech, but I was too sick to panic. I felt hands scooping me up. I saw a snatch of green. "Come, child. They want us to go into the canoes to take us to the shore. You have survived the journey. It is for a reason that one so young survived. Remember, child, you must live!"

The year was 1761. The month was July.

Long canoes brought us to shore. The captain led us to a large building, low and painted brown. People with pink faces, like the captain and the sailors, milled about and spoke loudly in the funny language that the captain spoke. Some pointed at our group of sickly captives. But I was surprised to see men and women who looked just like my people in Fouta and the Gambia. But how strangely they dressed! Some of these African-looking people shook their heads sorrowfully. Others quickly looked away from us.

As I write this, I am filled with a grief that will lurk forever beneath my skin. This sorrow plays hide-and-seek with me. Not my many poems that have been published, not all the accolades that I have received will heal this pain.

Years later, I would learn that as the ship sat in Boston Harbor, the captain, whose name was Gwinn, published news of his cargo in the local newspaper:

Just imported from Africa, a number of prime young slaves from the Windward Coast on the schooner Phillis. *They are to be sold at the dock at New Boston.*

Most of the captives of the *Phillis* were led onto the dock. A toubab man looked them up and down. A Serer man was told to step forward, his skin gleaming from the shea butter that the sailors had rubbed on him when we neared Boston. The toubab man told him to open his mouth, and he examined his teeth. The toubab told him to leap into the air. He told him to squat. He examined him the way my father examined a horse brought by Moorish traders on their annual caravans to Fouta.

"*Ladies and gentlemen,*" the toubab shouted. "*This Negro is in the prime of his life. He is around twenty-one years old and as strong as an ox. I will open the bidding for this Negro at eight hundred dollars. Do I hear a bid?*"

And so it was that our lives and freedom were auctioned away. Slave buyers and owners pushed through the noisy crowd and haggled for the healthy captives. They poked them all over their bodies. They examined their teeth, twisted their heads around, bent their limbs and made signs to jump up and down. Many of the captives, especially the children, began to weep.

The auction was boisterous. "*I'll buy that one for eight hundred and fifteen dollars,*" yelled a short man with a round face, pointing to a tall boy whom I knew to be a member of the royal family of the Serer.

"*No,*" replied the captain. "*He is worth a thousand. He is young and strong and has many productive years ahead of him.*"

I watched all this while lying on a piece of dirty rug in a corner of the dockyard with others who were very weak and sick. And there we stayed, trembling and crying. Captain Gwinn said that no one would buy us. We were the "refuse." We were left there to die. The angel with the green shawl ripped off a piece of the cloth and covered my trembling body. She held me and covered my face with kisses.

The loud wailing of two sisters caused me to look up. They spoke Fullah, the language of my people. "Sister, if we do not meet again in this world, we will meet in the next. God go with you." And the sisters held each other and wept before being dragged off by different buyers. Then the angel was dragged off by a man with a large, beefy face.

By mid-afternoon, the healthy captives had been sold. How long I lay on the dirty carpet I cannot say. I passed in and out of consciousness. Then I heard Captain Gwinn's voice.

"*Madam, she may not live long.*"

I roused myself and looked up into the face of a toubab woman with eyes the color of the sea. We locked our gaze for a long time, and then I heard her say, "*How much is she worth?*"

So it was that Susanna and John Wheatley bought me. Much later, Mrs. Wheatley told me that she had been very sick and confined to bed for a long time. When she recovered, her husband promised her a personal slave. The two domestics who had looked after my mistress and the household, Aunt Betty and Clara, were not as nimble as they used to be. Aunt Betty was arthritic and had problems climbing the stairs. Mistress needed a younger slave who could be trained as a domestic and who would walk in the way of the Lord. That was what had taken them to the market on that fateful day.

"We arrived late. By the time we got there, only the refuse slaves remained. My heart sank because I wanted an older teenager or someone in her early twenties, but all the slaves of that description were already sold."

Then they heard me whimpering. And they looked to see that the noise was coming from a child lying on a rug in a dimly lit corner. The Wheatleys' hearts were moved at the sight of her frail and emaciated body. "You will not want to buy her," the captain said.

"But your huge, sunken eyes revealed such sorrow and pain that I was immediately moved," my mistress told me. "We bought you for a mere trifle. Captain Gwinn told me you would die, so he sold you very cheaply. I wanted to prove him wrong. You are my miracle, Phillis."

My master was a rich merchant who owned two ships that traded with Britain, the West Indies and Nova Scotia. He also owned a store that sold wine, tea, coffee, rice, candles, dried fish, fish oil, fabric and a host of other items from around the world. The shop was in Boston's busy harbor. He employed a number of people to work on his ships and run his store. My master was also tailor to Boston's most distinguished people. His tailoring shop was on King Street, close to our house. He also owned several houses that he leased or rented.

My mistress helped me from the market to a small carriage. Though I was weak and my breath short, I could see that the driver of the carriage was an African. He smiled at me, and my heart felt a little comforted. He jumped from his seat, scooped me up and placed me on a soft seat at the back of the carriage. The driver's name was Prince, and he would become one of my guardians.

Prince guided the carriage along the dirt streets of Boston. My mistress would often look at me over her shoulder, from her seat at the front. A sigh would escape her lips. Finally, Prince opened the door and lifted me from my seat. I was looking up at a stately red-brick mansion. I could not but gasp at the size and grandeur of the house. It would be my home for the next seventeen years. I would later learn that the house stood at the intersection of King Street and Mackerel Lane, in the heart of the city, close to the sea but away from the docks.

<hr />

The long march to the coast and the sea journey would forever imprint my body and spirit. I became asthmatic. Sometimes, for days on end, my lungs would be shut tight against the air. But my body grew stronger and my spirit was calmed under the care of Mrs. Wheatley and Aunt Betty, the enslaved housekeeper. The Wheatleys' children, Mary and Nathaniel, were twins, fourteen years old. Instead of me caring for my mistress, my mistress cared for me in those first months. And she pressed Mary into service. The Wheatley women often read to me. They spoke kindly. They would point to me and say, "Phillis." I quickly realized it was my new name. Phillis, after the ship that brought me to America. Phillis. Penda was gone forever. They also gave me their last name. Penda Wane became Phillis Wheatley. What would my father think of my new name? He would not be able to fathom such a thing. Often I contemplated my new name as I drifted off to sleep at night. The thought of it broke my heart. But my master and mistress seemed to want to preserve my life, and as the days and the weeks rolled by, I came to accept my new name.

CHAPTER SEVEN

On the Wings of Morning

One day I knew I would not die. As I recovered, scenes of Fouta Toro rose sharply in my mind. Visiting my relatives, playing with my friends, making mischief on the cattle. Bathing in the river, playing with my baby sister, learning domestic chores from my mother. Sitting in our courtyard while my mother combed and braided her hair. Sitting beneath the village baobab tree reciting for Baba Dende, memorizing long passages, and Baba Dende getting upset and frustrated when we did not recite the way he wanted us to. Watching my father feed strips of cotton into his loom and marveling as he created a tapestry of stories from our history.

These memories nourished me, but they also made me extremely sad for a life I would never have again, never see again. So I commanded my mind to stop these memories. I was now in Boston, in toubab-land, in America, in the house of John and Susanna Wheatley, Nathaniel and Mary. I belonged to them. They would tell me what to do: when to wake up, when to go to bed, when to eat, what to eat, where to go, what to wear, how to talk and what to think. Yes, they would even tell me what to think, or if I should think at all.

In no time, I learned enough of the English tongue to speak to those around me. And after I gained sufficient health and strength, my training in household duties began. Aunt Betty, the housekeeper, taught me how to set the table, to sweep the house properly and to dust the furniture. She taught me to do light laundry. She also taught me how to serve meals and wait at the table. The work came easy because my mother had already been teaching me many of these things. Aunt Betty took me with her to the market and on errands for my mistress. But she did more than train me in household arts. She made special soups "to fatten me up." At night, Aunt Betty sang to me and told me stories of Brothers Rabbit, Tiger and Elephant and of Sister Deer. Aunt Betty had no children, and she hugged me and said, "God sent you to be my daughter, Phillis." And for that I rejoiced because though I had lost my own mother, God had rewarded me with two.

In addition to doing work around the house, I was to be Mrs. Wheatley's personal maid. I combed her hair, prepared her bath, fetched her clothes, made her bed, brought her meals if she felt too ill to dine with the family and ran errands for her. I also went to church with her, though I sat on the benches for Black people. Mistress was very pious and read the Bible a lot. Her favorite subject was talking about God.

God. Mistress and Aunt Betty spoke about God a lot. God seemed to be their special friend. They reminded me of Baba Dende, who also had God as his special friend. My mistress felt that if I came to know her God, I would be able to forget Africa. Every evening after supper, my mistress called us all together — the twins, my master, Aunt Betty, Prince, the two other house slaves, Rufus and Clara — for the bible reading and prayers. As soon as I knew enough English to understand, my mistress told me that a man named Jesus, a long, long time ago, had died for my sins. But I knew already about Jesus. My people revered him as a prophet.

But my mistress told me that I was a pagan, that Africa was a benighted land, and it was a good thing I had been brought into slavery because I could learn about the true God and his son, Jesus. I said nothing when my mistress and Mary made unflattering remarks about Africa, although I knew they were wrong. I had been happy there. I had lived a good life with my family. I had had plenty of food and drink and had been surrounded by love and laughter. And we knew that there was only one God, as my mistress was telling me.

A year passed, and I was speaking the English language fluently. I ventured to ask my mistress to teach me to write. And she did. I remembered Baba Dende under the baobab tree, scolding, frowning, encouraging, and my mind took flight.

"I daresay the child Phillis is very intelligent," my mistress said one day to my master after my lesson. "She learns faster than I can teach."

I smiled broadly. I was very pleased with myself. Mistress had once called me her "miracle," and she now set about proving that indeed I was. She and Mary began teaching me bible history, poetry, British history and classical literature.

One day, my mistress and Mary confessed that they had taught me all they knew. Nathaniel would have to become part of the great experiment. My young master was a student at Boston Latin

School, and he taught me Greek, Hebrew, Latin, theology, ancient history and rhetoric. After a few months of study, Nathaniel gave me Latin verses to translate into English. He introduced me to the poets Terence, Virgil, Horace and Catullus, though he said his teachers did not like Catullus much.

I soaked up all this learning. I became as familiar with Jesus turning water into wine as with Zeus hurling thunderbolts from Mount Olympus. Alexander Pope, the English poet, was as close a friend as was Terence Afer, the celebrated Roman playwright and an African. The gods and goddesses of antiquity peopled my imagination, and my heart would beat fast as I read about the English Revolution and how the English executed their king, Charles the First. But the Bible remained my favorite book. Reading it gave me strength, succor and inspiration. It eased some of the pain of the loss of my home and family. As I drank up the Wheatleys' learning, my mistress declared that I was a "prodigy." No one expected much from a mere slave, but here I was reading and writing in Latin. And speaking English better than many Whites, my mistress said. That pleased me greatly.

At that time I had no idea that what we were

doing was highly unusual. Slave owners normally did not teach their slaves to read or write, much less teach them Latin and Greek. Most felt that learning spoiled a slave because her natural condition was that of a servant. Learning put strange ideas in the mind of a slave and made her unfit for bondage.

My owners' amazement at the speed at which I learned made me realize that even they believed that Africans were not very intelligent. That is why I was a prodigy. But in Fouta Toro it was normal for young children to have memorized the entire Qur'an by the time they were eight. As for learning the English tongue fast, my country was a potpourri of languages. Most people, including my parents, spoke three or four languages apart from their mother tongue. Our ears were attuned to hearing and understanding. Those who came to trade in Tumbakulli spoke Bamana, Mandinka, Serer, Arabic, Songhai, Hassiniyya, Tuareg and a host of other tongues. My mind was open to learning a new and strange speech.

Oftentimes I found myself composing rhymes along the principles that my mother and Ma Ndiaye had taught me. Every other line rhymed;

every line had eight syllables. And then I would slip into the iambic pentameters and rhymes used by English poets. John Donne's Holy Sonnets filled my twelve-year-old heart with a sweet joy.

Batter my heart, three-person'd God; for you
As yet but knock, breathe, shine and seek to mend;
That I may rise and stand, o'erthrow me and bend
Your force, to break, blow, burn and make me new.

Or Pope's "Essay on Man."

Know then thyself, presume not God to scan;
The proper study of Mankind is Man.
Plac'd on this isthmus of a middle state,
A being darkly wise, and rudely great:
With too much knowledge for the Sceptic side,
With too much weakness for the Stoic's pride

Words I got from fetching my mistress's tea. From picking greens in the meadows with Aunt Betty and Prince, or with Rufus and Clara. Words I got conjugating Nathaniel's Latin verbs. Words I got from Mary's French songs. Words I got from Aunt Betty's stories. Words I got from the Bible and sermons preached by the pastors of Boston's churches. Words I got from my dreams. Words I got

from looking from my window in the early dawn
and seeing the sun breaking in the eastern sky.
Apollo heralding the dawn, Apollo escorting the sun.

Sometimes while I worked with Aunt Betty
mixing the batter for our bread, I would stop with
a piece of dough in my hand and stare into space.
"Phillis," Aunt Betty's voice would say. "Stop your
dreaming, child. We cannot eat air. Make the bread."
But I wasn't dreaming. I was listening to the words
speaking in my head.

Then, one evening, in the year I turned twelve,
it happened. At twilight I was sitting on a chair
in the room I shared with Aunt Betty. It was late
autumn and night came early. The room was filled
with an electric air and the words formed in
perfect meter and rhyme in my mind. It was as
if Ma Ndiaye was in the room, encouraging me,
coaxing me. Over and over the poem came,
without effort. I walked briskly to Mary's room
and I knocked.

Mary opened the door. "It is not time for lessons,
Phillis."

"I know, Miss Mary, but I need to borrow quill,
ink and paper. There is a poem in my head that I
must get out."

Mary gazed at me with a puzzled look, but a smile formed itself in the corners of her mouth.

And that was how it started and would not stop. Night or day, the poems poured out of me. Mary showed them to her mother. A few days later, my mistress moved me into a room of my own. A small bed was placed in one corner. There was a nightstand with washbasin. But what caught my eye was the desk. It had an inkwell and stacks of paper. I held the papers between my fingers and chills ran over my body. A strange, sweet sensation. The desk was placed beside the window, giving me a full view of the street and much light. My own room. My room with a desk.

"From now on, Phillis, no more sharing with Betty," my mistress informed me. I loved the comfort of Aunt Betty's companionship. I would miss her stories and warmth; but we would still work together, cooking, cleaning, dusting and serving.

But then my mistress told me that I must not associate with the other slaves, nor was I to "play" with them or engage in jokes. Mistress told me that I was "superior" to them and to all the slaves in Boston. Since I was so educated, I should not dally with ignorant people.

Her words hit me like a hammer. Aunt Betty, Prince, Rufus and Clara were my family. They looked out for me and took care of me. Though Aunt Betty could not read, she was not "uneducated." She knew lots of stories and songs and was the best cook and baker in all of Massachusetts. But I had no say in how my mistress directed my life. Loneliness would be the price I had to pay for becoming a learned woman. The Wheatleys poured their knowledge into me, and my enforced separation from my fellows began.

My favorite time to write was in the early morning, when not a soul stirred, and in the evening at twilight. Baba Dende once told the class that the angels visit and listen to our hearts during these periods. Yes, that must be true. Because when night turns into day, and day turns into night, I am filled with such peace and sweet feeling. During those moments, the space inside of me becomes filled with a glow that grows larger and larger until it fills all of me and then surrounds me and fills the entire room. In these moments, the words come easily and I feel blessed and protected.

One morning, as I lit my lamp, I heard a soft knock.

"It's me, Phillis." I opened my door and there stood Aunt Betty holding a candle, smiling broadly. Though I called her "Aunt" and she cared for me like a mother, she never spoke to me in the patronizing manner in which most adults speak to children. There was complete ease between us. But we had to be careful. Mistress would get very angry if she knew Aunt Betty and I still met and spoke, however briefly.

"I stopped to see if you were up. I will bring you something to eat." Aunt Betty disappeared and came back in no time with a tray. She walked in the dark because she knew the house like the back of her hand. Aunt Betty handed me the tray and kissed my forehead. "God bless you, my daughter." I returned her blessing with a smile.

In between my duties, I wrote verses. Sometimes, when my mistress sent me on an errand in town, a poem would burst in my head. The words would spin over and over, and as soon as I got home I would rush to write them down, the words coming faster than my fingers could write. I wrote poems that I would never show my owners, poems about Senegal and the life I would never have again. Poems about slavery and the wrongness of it. Poems that demand we all breathe a free air. I kept these poems hidden beneath my mattress.

Yet I knew I was fortunate. Other young slaves in Boston were regularly whipped, had to sleep outdoors and were never given enough to eat. Some who displeased their owners were shipped to the sugar plantations of the Caribbean, or to the tobacco farms of Virginia and Maryland, to toil in the burning sun with little to eat and slave drivers whipping them.

Some of these poems came to me because I would wander down to the harbor while on errands. If a cargo of captive Africans was there, my eyes invariably sought out the refuse captives. I remembered when I, too, lay on a dirty rug, forgotten by all. The scene made the old terror and helplessness rise in my soul, and I would have to turn away to control my shaking and rage. Another thing about this forlorn scene impressed itself on my mind, and it was that these African captives must have seen me as a strangely dressed African in the same way I saw the American Blacks when I first landed in Boston.

CHAPTER EIGHT

The Making of a Poet

My first poem to be published was "On Messrs Hussey and Coffin." It told the story of two Nantucket gentlemen who were on their way to Boston when their ship sailed into a hurricane off Cape Cod. They narrowly escaped death. The Wheatleys invited the two men to dinner one evening, and as I served them I heard them tell their story. Shipwrecked and near death. I knew these well from my journey on the slave ship *Phillis*. In my mind's eye, I saw their ship pushed to and fro by Boreas, the god of the north wind, and Eolus, king of the four winds. Even as I served the gentlemen, the poem formed in my mind. At the close of the evening, the words simply flowed through my fingers onto paper.

Did fear and danger so perplex your Mind,
As made you fearful of the Whistling Wind?
Was it not Boreas knit his angry Brow

Against you? or did Consideration bow?
To lend you Aid, did not his Winds combine?
To stop your passage with a churlish line,
Did haughty Eolus with Contempt look down
With Aspect windy, and a study'd Frown?

My mistress was so impressed that she sent the poem to several New England newspapers. *The Newport Mercury* of Rhode Island published it on 21 December 1767. I was thirteen years old. Soon all of Boston was speaking of the "Negro poetess, slave of Mr. Wheatley."

I wrote poem after poem. Mistress was proud of my achievements and organized small readings and performance parties for the cream of Boston society. My first reading was at the Wheatleys'. Mistress and Master invited a few guests, among them Governor Thomas Hutchinson and the distinguished Reverend Samuel Cooper (our next-door neighbor). I was nervous, but Mistress told me to believe in the power of my own verse, and the guests were encouraging.

It was one thing to read to the Wheatleys, but quite another to read in front of others. My tongue felt like lead in my mouth. Nervousness made me read in a squeaky voice. But that did not seem to matter. What mattered was that I, a slave, had written the poems. Many found this unbelievable, and most thought of me as an oddity, as my mistress's great experiment: the slave who was a poet. The slave who recited poetry. What a curiosity!

But many people were kind. Reverend Cooper gave me a book of John Donne's poetry, and Governor Hutchinson gave me a text on rhetoric. Invitations abounded for me to give recitals in the homes of Boston's finest. Sometimes, my mistress or master received a small sum of money for my performances. In the summer, when the Wheatleys, like other fashionable Bostonians, retired to Newport to escape Boston's stifling heat, I gave readings in the homes of Newport's high society. Yet, for all the adulation, though I was a "genius," I was still an African, a slave, and not their equal. How could they say I had a "superior" mind and then refuse me a place at their dining table? The slaves took great pleasure in my recitals. They were proud of me and told me so. But mistress said I was superior to other slaves and forbade me to eat with them. I could eat neither with the Whites nor with the Blacks.

Some of the recitals were monstrous, like my reading at the Fitches'. Even before I left my house my heart was heavy. There they were: Mr. and Mrs. Fitch, their three teenage daughters and four guests. The servant was pouring them tea, and they were all making merry. Mrs. Fitch offered me tea, but I did not accept it. I told her that I was ready to read, that I had to leave soon because I had a later engagement. That was not true, but I wanted to get out of the house as soon as possible.

I hurried through each poem, watching Mrs. Fitch and her daughters. They drank their tea and ate tea cakes, laughing and touching one another's hands. I wanted to puke. Mr. Fitch must have read my thoughts because I saw him whisper to his wife; then she did the same to each daughter. Their laughter and chatter ceased — but only for an instant. And in that instant I knew that they *knew*. I wanted to take the hot tea and hurl it at them.

Instead, I finished my reading and told Mrs. Fitch I had to leave. But the wretched woman offered me tea. "No, ma'am," I said quite loudly, "I do not wish for tea." She turned beet red. How could she offer me tea when her husband had told her that he owned the ship that brought me to this country? Yes, Mr. Fitch owned the *Phillis*. And it was my labor and that of countless other Africans stolen from their mothers' bosoms and their fathers' embraces that enabled the Fitches to live in a fine home with fine furniture, treat their daughters like pets and embrace them each and every morning. *No, ma'am, I do not want tea.* I want to be with my mother, as you are with your daughters. I want to eat sweetmeats and yogurt with my mother, as you drink tea and eat tea cakes with your daughters.

An uncomfortable silence descended on the living room. I took up the satchel holding my precious poems, bade the Fitches and their guests *adieu* and descended to the street, where Prince waited with the coach. I climbed in and began telling him what had happened at the Fitches'.

In my anger and grief I forgot the rules. Not only did I talk to Prince, but I sat with him at the front of the coach all the way home. Mistress ran from the house and screamed at Prince. "Why are you sitting beside *my* Phillis? Never, never seat her beside you. She is too good for you!" As my mistress's little pet, I was caught between the free and the slave, not good enough for one set and "too good" for the other. My only friend was my own heart. I poured my loneliness into poetry.

Almost every month, one of my poems appeared in a paper in New England, Philadelphia or New York. My fame spread. I was "Phillis Wheatley, the African poet," "Phillis Wheatley, the African genius," "Phillis Wheatley, Boston's slave poet." If I said that I was not pleased by the fame and attention, I would be lying, because I was thrilled every time I saw my name and poem in print. I only wished that my mother, my father and all those who raised me in Fouta could see my achievements. What would Baba Dende say? Would he be pleased that I had conquered the language of the toubab? Would my mother be happy that I had become a griot like her, if not in the language of her people?

❧

It was not until I met Obour Tanner that I realized how I had missed a close relationship with someone my own age. The White children looked down on me. Most of the Black children I saw came with their owners to Sunday services. and my mistress forbade me to talk to them. Servant children often came to our house on errands, but our interaction was brief and to the point. I met Obour when I was fifteen years old, during my owners' summer vacation in Newport. Obour was from Providence, but came down to Newport with her mistress. Obour was my own age, tall, slim and ebony-colored. She could have been from my own country, but Obour was born in Rhode Island. She spoke like the Americans.

Obour was with her mistress one evening when I gave a reading at the home of Jacob Perez. Like most Newport merchants, Mr. Perez made his money from the slave trade. Some of it he invested in the whaling trade. He was the richest man in all of Rhode Island, but I was not impressed by blood money.

Obour was standing behind the White audience, of course. I saw this girl who looked just like me. I gasped. She must have read my thoughts because she smiled from across the room.

After the reading, Obour came over to me.

"They call you the African genius." My face grew hot. Obour must have seen my discomfort because she quickly added, "No need to be embarrassed. They are right. You must be a genius to write like that." I said nothing, but she continued. "Let's walk at the back of the house. I know your mistress does not like you to talk to us." We escaped through the back door and strolled in the parklike grounds.

"Who is Phoebus?" Obour asked.

"Another name for Apollo, the sun god of the ancient Greeks and Romans."

"Recite that one again."

"Which one?"

"The one about the Gambia, where you compare Africa to the Garden of Eden."

I needed no prompting.

The Various bower, the tuneful flowing stream,
The soft retreats, the lovers' golden dream;
Her soil spontaneous, yields exhaustless stores;
For Phoebus revels on her verdant shores
Whose flowery births a fragrant train appear,
And Crown the youth throughout the smiling years.

Obour clapped her hands and laughed. "I wish I could write poetry."

"But you can."

"No."

"Then you can do other things."

And with that she brightened. "I can sew. In fact, I'm very good at it. See the dress my mistress is wearing? I made it."

Everyone had admired the stylish dress, but the expression on my face must have told Obour of my disbelief.

"That is why my mistress has employed me. Because I can sew and read. She said she did not want an ignorant servant."

I must have looked confused. I thought Obour was a slave. She read my mind.

"I am free. I work for a wage."

"You grew up in Providence?"

"No, I am from Smithfield. I came to Providence to work for my mistress. I like Providence. Smithfield is all farms. Lots of cows. All country."

I laughed out loud, remembering the cattle in Fouta that we children threw stones at. "Our people adore cattle," I told Obour. "My brother Amadi had a name for each of his cows."

"So you are a true African? Born in Africa?" she

asked. I nodded and braced for the inevitable insults, but instead she said, "Tell me about your country," her voice filled with curiosity.

I coaxed my stifled memories from the recesses of my mind. First, about the cows. As I spoke, a floodgate opened and the memories flew from my heart, onto my tongue and into Obour's ears. I felt giddy with relief. For the first time, I could speak about myself without feeling ashamed or stupid. I loved my mistress dearly, but she had taught me to mask my true self. I did try. Tried to forget my past, my country, pushing every memory down, down. So much so that my mistress said that my grammar, my speech and my deportment were as excellent, yea, even better than those of a White girl. "The only thing that does not make you White, Phillis, is your skin," my mistress remarked with pride and a little disappointment. I had felt flattered by my mistress's words, until their full meaning hit me like a stone.

Obour gave me back a piece of myself I thought I had lost forever, a piece I would always conceal from my mistress and other Whites.

"How did you learn to read, Obour?" I asked, coming back to the present moment.

"From my father. He was a sailor. He sailed the seven seas," she said proudly.

"Was he a free man?"

"No ... and yes. He belonged to John Brown, the wealthiest merchant in all New England. That's how he became a sailor. He began as a slave on one of John Brown's whaling ships when he was twelve. Later he joined the pirates. Yes, on a pirate ship. Pirates share the booty equally, you know. That's how my father bought his freedom. They plundered ships from almost every nation."

"He must have seen many things," I said, impressed.

"Yes. He speaks Portuguese, Spanish and French. That's how he met my mother. She was a Portuguese African."

Obour's story was taking on a touch of the fantastical.

"It's true, Phillis. When my father was a pirate, they captured a ship in the Atlantic bound for Brazil. It was a ship from Portugal. On board were all these rich Portuguese people with their slaves and servants. My mother was called Caterina Teresa, and she was slave to a very rich lady connected to the Portuguese court. My mother made all of her clothes. She was an expert seamstress. Her specialty was embroidery.

"The New England pirates towed the captured ship to Newport and took the cargo and all the gold and jewelry. Eventually, the rich Portuguese were ransomed, along with their slaves; but by that time my mother and father had fallen in love, and she refused to go to Brazil. Her mistress could not force her, you see, on account of being a hostage. So my mother remained in Rhode Island. My father gave up the sea, and since he was still technically a slave of John Brown, he bought his freedom, married my mother, and they started a farm in Smithfield."

Obour and I became fast friends. We wrote to each other after we left Newport each summer — she to Providence and I to Boston. And every summer we would reunite when my owners and her employers sailed to Newport for their vacations.

Part of our friendship was our shared love of religion. Both of us were Christians. Once I had learned English, my mistress insisted I become a Christian. Our bible studies were designed to teach me the principles of Christianity. When I turned twelve, I began taking instruction from Reverend Cooper at the South End Church. However, it was my mistress's story about the resurrection of a dead girl by Jesus that opened my heart to her faith.

Mistress told me that Jesus was a special friend of children. She said he loved them more than he loved any other people. And to illustrate this point, she told me the story of the rich man and his daughter.

Once there was a rich man who loved his daughter more than his own life. But one day she fell sick and died. The rich man pounded his chest and asked God why he had taken his only child. Knowing that Jesus could perform miracles, the rich man told him about the death of his daughter, weeping as he did so.

"Go home," Jesus said to the man.

"You're not coming with me?" the rich man asked.

"No. Go home."

The rich man was annoyed with Jesus and told him so, but Jesus replied, "Your child lives. Your faith has resurrected your daughter. Now go in peace."

The rich man hurried back to his house and found his daughter not only alive, but well.

When my mistress related the story, I saw myself as the rich man's daughter, lost to her father through slavery. But unlike the rich man, my father had lost me forever. I wept for the pain of it.

Mistress was puzzled; then a light of understanding flickered in her eyes. She hugged me and said, "God is your heavenly father, Phillis, and through him you are found and born anew."

Shortly after, Reverend Cooper baptized me, and I became a steadfast believer, although it was Reverend George Whitefield, the English pastor, whom everyone credited with starting "The Great Awakening."

Reverend Whitefield tramped through the Thirteen Colonies, taking his message to all who would listen, and thousands flocked to hear him. Africans, Indians and Whites got the spirit when the Reverend preached, and he baptized them all. I, too, heard Reverend Whitefield preach. He did not hold, as did many others, that receiving the Gospel was a privilege. "We are all entitled to God's grace and mercy," he said. When he came to Boston, the crowd was so thick that the church could not hold everyone. So we all marched to the common, which was big and wide and had room for all.

He preached that God would punish us if we did not repent. He said that God does not distinguish between persons — Black, White, Indian, mixed bloods, man, woman, master, slave, child, American or British. He said that God sees our hearts, not our garments or skin. He said that every person is equal in the sight of God and that on the day of judgment each of us will be called to give account of our deeds. His fiery preachings were talked about all over New England.

The Sunday after Reverend Whitefield preached in Boston, Reverend Byles gave a sermon in his Congregational church insisting that it was wrong for Reverend Whitefield to claim that all the races were equal. Obour and I held our sides and laughed when we met in Newport the following summer and I told her how Reverend Byles had got in a fit over Mr. Whitefield preaching to "mixed" audiences and saying we "are all equal in God's sight."

What Reverend Whitefield preached was new, and it struck the ear as odd. No priest or pastor in

Boston had ever preached such an idea. Boston's clerics told the Indian and African servants to obey their masters and be good slaves. They said that distinctions based on color were a natural part of God's creation and should be adhered to.

My mistress knew the Reverend Whitefield and, whenever he was in Boston, invited him to dine with us. They had a mutual friend, Selina Hastings, the Countess of Huntingdon, an English noble-woman who used her fortune to train, hire and send preachers, mainly of the Methodist persuasion, all over the world. Though Lady Huntingdon belonged to the Anglican Church, she believed staid rituals suited only the rich. She used her money to enable pastors like Mr. Whitefield to preach in every nook and cranny to every race. Reverend Whitefield was the countess's personal chaplain, and my mistress supported the countess's religious causes in New England and elsewhere.

Once, when Reverend Whitefield dined with us, my mistress also had Reverend Samson Occom, a Methodist preacher, at our table. The countess gave financial support to Reverend Occom to do missionary work among his people, the Mohican

Indians. The Wheatleys also helped Reverend Occom in his work.

Reverend Whitefield was an outspoken man. Even at the Wheatley dinner table, he said that slavery was evil, that it was wrong for one race to hold another in bondage. Neither my master nor my mistress responded, but his words were not lost on them. I prayed for Reverend Whitefield every night. I also prayed for his benefactress, Lady Huntingdon.

The reverend had a powerful voice, which drew many into the circle of salvation. But he suffered from asthma. His journeys throughout the length and breadth of America, Britain and the West Indies took their toll. In September 1770, after preaching in New Hampshire, the great man had a severe attack of asthma. He knew the Lord was calling him home, and he died soon after.

I felt the loss deeply. Other than the Wheatley family, he was one of the few Whites who saw me as a person of worth. In one of his orations on Boston Common, he had warned that if America and Britain did not stop their slave-holding and slave-dealing ways, robbing Africa of its sons and daughters, a great catastrophe would come upon them. He had said what I could not say, and for that I loved him.

So on his passing I wrote a poem in his memory, an elegy for the great preacher. Little did I know that writing this lament would change my life.

The poem flew from my pen like the currents of a river, and when I was through it ran to twenty-three pages. Even I was surprised. I showed it to my mistress, and she showed it to my master. He took it to a Boston printer and got it published as a broadside and also as a pamphlet. All of Boston loved it. Printers in Philadelphia and New York also published it. And the poem quickly sold out. Then I had an idea — why not send a copy to Lady Huntingdon and attach a letter of condolence expressing my grief about the passing of Mr. Whitefield? And that was what I did.

CHAPTER NINE

The Examination

In January 1771, to my great pleasure, the countess wrote back. She thanked me for the poem and letter, and then told me that she had had the elegy published in a London newspaper! I could not believe my eyes. Now, on both sides of the great Atlantic, people read my poetry! *My* poetry!

The publication of my elegy to Reverend Whitefield made my master and mistress think about publishing my poems in book form. I had written more than one hundred poems on religious and moral matters. But even though almost everyone in Boston called me a "prodigy" and a "genius," my master could not find a printer to publish my book. Even though I had read poetry in the parlors of many of Boston's finest, they still felt unsure that a Black slave child could be so gifted. They believed that I was not authentic, that an African could not possibly *write*, much less write poetry. "Did she really write these poems? How can we be sure?

We have never heard of a Black person creating literature."

I was crushed. I had read like a monkey in the drawing rooms of these hypocrites, composed poems about their dead relatives, for whom I cared little, and now they questioned my gift, my talent, my genius. No matter how brilliant I was, it would never be enough for these people. It did not matter that I had lost my mother tongue and mastered their own, that I spoke and wrote it better than they. So blinded were they by their prejudice that they could ask, "Did she write this?" Jealousy, that's what it was. They were jealous that I was more gifted than they.

My master and mistress knew that I was the authoress of the poems. They were the ones who had schooled and tutored me. They knew that their "African genius" was real. My master tried to soften the blow. He told me that Boston's publishers did not doubt my abilities, but that in order to publish any book they needed at least two hundred buyers to commit to purchase a copy once it was printed. That way the publisher was assured of making at least a small profit. But Master's explanation made me even angrier. Most Bostonians knew of my talents and ought to have subscribed. Just when I wished to step out farther into the world, they wished to push me back. It was one thing for a slave to write and read poems, it was quite another for her to have an actual book published. Boston would thwart the aspirations of any ambitious slave.

"This is what we will do, Phillis," my master said to me one afternoon as I served him tea. His plan was brilliant, and we set it in motion. On 7 October 1772, I would be examined by eighteen good gentlemen of Boston. Their objective? To see if indeed I was the authoress of the verses my master said I had written. These distinguished men were to examine my learning, then decide if my verses had been written by me. If they concluded that I was authentic, I would be vindicated, and we could find a publisher. Or so we thought.

I dressed carefully on the day. My mistress chose a yellow silk dress with a dark green collar. My bonnet was of simple white cotton. My mistress and I read verses from the Bible. I was not nervous and ate all my breakfast. I took seventeen poems in my satchel. The meeting was to take place at State House, in the office of the governor. If the committee decided that I had written the poems, not only I but the entire Black race would be vindicated.

Many Whites feel that slavery is the natural condition of Black people. That we are inferior and cannot create great literature or science. I wonder at this ridiculous reasoning. Every race produces its great men and women. To those who say that Africans cannot produce great things, have they not heard of the great empires of Ghana, and Mali, and Songhai? Of ancient Egypt? To those who say the Africans cannot create literature, I say, "Lies!" The great Terence, an African slave in Rome, was a master playwright and essayist.

After praying with my mistress, I sat in my room for a long while. The pitcher on the washstand beckoned me. As I poured water into the basin, I remembered the pools of the river of my homeland. I remembered my mother making her ablutions before she prayed and teaching me to make mine. So, as she taught me, I washed my face, my hands, the inside of my mouth. I wiped my hair with the water and, with wet hands, brushed against my feet. Then I recited the prayers that Baba Dende had taught us.

I was ready.

At the State House, the seat of Massachusetts' government, I was ushered into a wide room in which hung portraits of the founding fathers of the colony. I looked at that of Cotton Mather, the stern Puritan who taught that the Indians were savages and that it was right to subjugate them. He thought little better of women, whatever their race.

At the large and circular table in front of me sat eighteen of the colony's first citizens. Among them was the colony's governor, Thomas Hutchinson. Beside him was Andrew Oliver, the lieutenant-governor. I recognized John Hancock, one of Boston's wealthiest merchants; the Reverend Mather Byles of the Hollis Street Congregational Church; and Mr. Thomas Hubbard, a rich slave trader. A smile played at the corner of Reverend Cooper's mouth. Surely *he* knew that I had written the poems. He had given me books to encourage my work as a poet; he had baptized me. But I could not take anything for granted. These were powerful and influential men. Their words carried weight. They all had taken degrees at Harvard College. Like Mr. Hubbard, several were slave owners.

They sat around the table in their dark suits with

their eyeglasses perched at the tips of their white noses, their wigs covering their ears. They peered at me, and I felt exposed. My mistress was always telling me to eat more because I was so slim. She also told me not to stand too much in the sun, because I was already "too dark." Standing before these men, I felt skinny, but my dark skin covered me like a warm, soft blanket. Yet my heart flipped-flopped. I was there not only to defend myself as the author of my poems, but also to defend the intelligence of my people. If I failed, they would say, "See, we told you that Blacks are not smart. How can such a lowly race master the art of literature?" Such a responsibility pressed down on my young shoulders. Suddenly I felt scared and wanted to run from the room. Run from these comfortable men. But then I remembered my mother praising me when I memorized a long ancestral praise poem, Baba Dende encouraging me as I recited and my mistress, Susanna Wheatley, marveling at my intelligence. My heart settled down. I was ready to answer any questions these men might pose.

A servant brought in a small chair and desk with paper, quill and ink. The governor began the examination. He asked me to recite parts of Homer's

Odyssey in Greek. I did. The mayor asked me questions on British history. I answered correctly. Reverend Mather Byles told me to compose poems in Latin. That I did and passed the verses to him. He read and passed them to his fellow examiners. A murmuring erupted around the table. Reverend Cooper asked me to translate prose from Latin into English, and he handed me the paragraph. I worked assiduously and handed the translated paragraph to him. One by one, each man asked me questions or set some test. They asked me if I could read before I arrived in America. I wanted to say yes, that my teacher, Baba Dende, had taught me my Arabic letters, but instead I said, "No."

"So your master and his family taught you all you know?"

"Yes."

"When did you begin to write poetry?"

"I was about ten years old."

"Are you a Christian, my child?"

The question almost made me laugh. I looked at Reverend Cooper, and his eyes twinkled. "Yes, sir. I am baptized, but have been a believer since I came to these shores."

My master, who had been quiet all along, spoke

up. "She is now a member of our church, the South End Meeting Hall."

After what seemed like an eternity, the men told me to wait in the outer room. A servant brought me tea and biscuits. The examination had been long and strenuous, and I was hungry. However, I felt serene. I knew the men had the power to decide my future life, but I had done my best. I had answered well the questions they had asked me. After a while, the door swung wide open and I saw my master striding toward me, his head held high. And I knew even before he opened his mouth. He smiled broadly. "Congratulations, Phillis. You have passed!" My master could not contain his glee. I clapped my hands. I felt the tears brimming in my eyes.

"Wait a minute, Phillis," my master said and stepped back through the door of the examination room. After what seemed like an eternity, he returned and waved a piece of paper at me.

"We cannot leave without this."

I did not know if I should laugh or cry, for what I experienced on reading it was both pain and pleasure. The eighteen examiners had given my master a certificate of authentication. They verified that indeed Phillis Wheatley was a poet. But it is how they wrote it:

> *We whose Names are under-written, do assure the*
> *World, that the POEMS specified in the following*
> *Page, were (as we verily believe) written by*
> *PHILLIS, a young Negro Girl, who was but a few*
> *Years since, brought an uncultivated Barbarian*
> *from Africa, and has ever since been, and now is,*
> *under the Disadvantage of serving as a Slave in a*
> *Family in this Town. She has been examined by*
> *some of the best Judges, and is thought qualified*
> *to write them.*

I felt the anger boiling in me. After that grueling examination, they still refused to say that they *knew* I was the author of the poems. Instead they said that they *believed* I wrote them. So the doubt lingered. And they said I was brought a barbarian from Africa. How dare they! Barbarism I had discovered in White people. The shackling of the slaves, the theft of their labor, the beatings and whippings, the horror of the sea journey from West Africa to Massachusetts — that was barbarism. In my native land I learned manners and respect for my elders, was taught to care for those weaker than myself, learned honesty and gentleness, learned justice, learned how to be a human in a community of humans. How dare they!

And yet I knew their words meant much. If they said they believed I wrote the poems, others would believe them, too. Who would doubt the words of men as distinguished as the governor and as venerable as Reverend Byles?

"Phillis, it is good," my master said, noting the expression on my face. I looked up and smiled at him.

"Yes, sir. It is good."

But for all my hard work and the grueling examination, I still had no publisher. Boston had rejected me and, through me, my master and mistress. In order to convince the public of the authenticity of my poetic talents, my master saw fit to publish a letter in a local paper.

Phillis was brought from Africa to America, in the Year 1761, between Seven and Eight years of age. Without any assistance from school education, and by only what was taught in the family, she, in sixteen months' time from her arrival, attained the English Language, to which she was an utter stranger before, to such a degree, as to read the most difficult parts of the sacred writings, to the great astonishment of all who heard her.

As to her writing, her own curiosity led her to it; and this she learnt in so short a time, that in the year 1765 she wrote a letter to Rev. Mr. Occom, the Indian minister.

She has a great inclination to learn the Latin tongue, and has made some progress in it. This relation is given by her master who bought her, and with whom she now lives.

But my mistress would not wait for Boston. She remembered that I had sent the pious Lady Huntingdon a copy of the elegy I had written on the death of Reverend Whitefield, and that the countess had published the poem in the London papers. Why not ask the countess for help?

If there was one person in the world who knew that Blacks could create literature, it was the countess, because it was she who had published the autobiographical narrative of James Gronniosaw, an African like myself who had been taken into slavery. Mr. Gronniosaw's book was titled *Narrative of the Most Remarkable Particulars in the*

Life of James Albert Ukawsaw Gronniosaw, an African Prince, as Related by Himself. Mr. Gronniosaw showed by the writing of his book that indeed the African could write.

His book had caused a stir in Boston. It was reviewed in all the leading papers, and my heart said, "Yes, yes! Bless him, oh my God," because Mr. Gronniosaw had used his pen as a mighty sword. I would have loved to purchase his book, but I could not afford it.

So my mistress wrote to the countess and asked for help. The countess wrote back to my mistress telling her to send me to England. When we received the countess's letter, we could not contain our excitement. Me, going to England?

"I will send you with Nathaniel," my mistress announced. "He is to go to England to look after some family business. He is to travel on our ship, the *London Packet*."

And so it was decided.

CHAPTER TEN

In London Town

On 17 June 1773, I stood with my young master Nathaniel on the dock of Boston Harbor. I was to travel once more across the Atlantic, not into slavery but as a celebrated poet.

The first few days at sea filled me with terror, and at nights I suffered the torments of nightmare: Captain Gwinn and his sailors whipping the captives, little Jibril dying beside me and being fed to the sharks. One night I screamed so loudly that the first officer ran to my cabin and pounded on the door. His banging woke me, and I realized that I was not on a slave ship. I called to him that I was all right, and he went away. But a few moments later, there was a loud knock on my door.

"Phillis, it's me, Nathaniel. Mr. Sinclair said you were upset."

I rose from my bunk, bile in my throat, and opened the door.

"What is it, Phillis?" he asked. "Are you homesick?"

I smiled weakly and tried to assure Nathaniel that I was fine. But the lie stuck in my throat. Tears coursed down my face. "I dreamed that I was on the slave ship."

"I suspected as much." Nathaniel entered the cabin and sat on the chair close to my bunk. "Phillis, you are not on a slave ship. Don't be afraid. The ship is taking you to London, the center of the world, where your book will be published and you will become even more famous than you are."

The presence of Nathaniel was enough to make me feel better. He had been a true friend from the moment I set foot in the Wheatley household. It was he who taught me Latin and ancient history. It was he who told me about Africa, Morocco and Hausa. He showed me my country on the map of the world.

"I do understand, Phillis, I do," he continued.

Nathaniel is good and kind, but no one who had not been on *that* journey could understand. Nathaniel rose up from his seat. "It is still night, and I must get my rest. Promise me you will be all right. If anything happened to you, my mother would not forgive me."

"I will be fine, I promise you."

My young master then took my hand, looked

me in the eye and said, "All will be well, Phillis."

I realized then how much I loved Nathaniel.

The journey proceeded without disturbance until we were off the coast of Newfoundland. "Whales, whales!" the cry went up. Everyone gathered on deck to see those mammoth creatures. One came right up to the ship's stern and swam alongside. Then he raised himself, looked directly in my eyes and spewed water on me. The people on deck cheered. Captain Caleb told me that sailors believed that seeing whales brings good luck.

The countess sent one of her confidants, Brook Watson, to meet us at the pier in London. I would be staying with her, while Nathaniel had secured lodgings for himself. If I thought Boston was busy, London was ten times more so. Our carriage rushed through the streets, and I believed that I would breathe my last breath as it nearly collided with oncoming carriages.

Vendors hawked their wares, pedestrians — some of whom were street urchins — rushed about, bawling at the top of their lungs. The buildings were ten times taller than those in Boston, which, for the longest while, I had believed was the center of the world.

The rains for which London is famous began.

They did not cool the air. They only increased the humidity, and soon sweat was pouring from my body.

The countess was what I had imagined her to be. Her skin was alabaster white, and her gray eyes sparkled. She walked briskly from her house to meet the carriage. Mr. Watson helped me down, and the countess pressed her hand in mine. "Phillis Wheatley, the famous poet." I immediately liked her.

The days blurred into one another, a mass of new faces and new places. One day, the much-esteemed Granville Sharp escorted me to the London Zoo. Mr. Sharp is famous for his efforts to bring about the end of the slave trade. There is an anti-slavery society in London, of which Mr. Sharp is the leader. He and his associates have presented many petitions to Parliament documenting the vile practices of slavery and the slave trade and calling for the end of these twin horrors. Just last year Mr. Sharp made history. He rescued James Somersett, a New England slave, from sure bondage. Somersett had travelled to England with his master. In 1771, he escaped from his master but was promptly recaptured and put on a ship bound for Jamaica. Sharp obtained legal representation for

Somersett, and the case was heard in the highest court of the land.

The judge, Lord Mansfield, ruled in Somersett's favor and released him. He said that "whoever breathes the air of England is a free man." What a triumph for Somersett, Sharp and the anti-slavery cause! Yet hundreds, if not thousands, of my brethren remained in bondage in Britain.

Mr. Sharp came for me in a cab. As we rumbled along the London streets, he tried to engage me in conversation, but I was tongue-tied in the presence of such an esteemed personage. However, he was a kind and sympathetic man, and he knew how to make me feel at ease. He asked about the situation at home in America, the strained relationship between the colonists and the government representative.

"I hear the Americans are talking about separating from Britain and becoming independent," he said. It was a subject close to my heart, and I needed no further encouragement to tell him how I felt. The colonists had legitimate complaints. Why should they be taxed without authentic representatives in the House of Parliament? Why should the British treat the Americans in a high-handed manner?

"But independence, Miss Wheatley?"

"The Americans see themselves as slaves ..."

Mr. Sharp and I looked at each other and smiled broadly. "I have been reading the rhetoric," he said. "I also read your poem to Lord Dartmouth."

"Though, sir, the real slaves are us, the Africans."

"No man of sense can miss that paradox," Mr. Sharp said, almost to himself.

"Britain is the best friend of the slave," I said passionately. "Look at your work for James Somersett and for England's Black slaves. Lady Huntingdon, God bless her soul, took me under her wing and enabled my book to be published, while Boston is still skeptical about an African poet."

"Such a pity."

"They believe, Mr. Sharp, that the African does not have the capacity for mental reasoning, higher thoughts and the writing and creating of literature and mathematics. They were not convinced that I had written the poems."

"There is much work to be done in fighting bigotry against the African, Miss Wheatley," he said. "Your work and your presence here in England have done much to advance the cause of your injured race."

At the zoo, I saw animals of every type and size, from the almost-white Siberian tiger to the South American yellow butterfly. There were also animals from my country: lions, elephants and zebras. I looked at these animals in their cages, behind their bars, and sent them a silent hello.

It was while looking at the tigers that Mr. Sharp said, "You know, Miss Wheatley, if you were to stay in London, you would gain your freedom. We, your friends here, would help you."

My heart beat fiercely. "I know, sir. I know."

It was hot and humid in London. The stifling heat sapped my energy, though Amelia, my maid, made me consume glass after glass of lemonade. Still, I visited museums, art galleries, the port of London and the big palaces: Buckingham, Whitehall and Hampton Court. But the Tower of London was the most fascinating. Benjamin Franklin, the much-regarded American politician, scientist and patriot, took me to the tower. Mr. Franklin had received many accolades for his work with electricity. He had read of my visit to London and the imminent publication of my book and, in a flush of patriotism, this good gentleman decided to visit me. I had been at my desk writing a letter to Obour Tanner when Amelia came to my room and told me that a gentleman named "Mr. Benjamin Franklin of Philadelphia" was here to visit me. I could not believe my ears.

"Welcome to England, Miss Wheatley," Mr. Franklin said, taking off his hat and bowing. He looked just like his engraving, which so often graced the pages of our American papers, with a large forehead and twinkling eyes. I thanked Mr. Franklin for his visit, but before I could conclude, he said, "I hope you are not being cooped up in the house. London has many sites that we colonials find fascinating. They are all meant to impress us, you know." Mr. Franklin laughed at his own comments, and I smiled. "I know Mr. Sharp took you to the zoo."

"Word does travel, Mr. Franklin," I exclaimed.

"Blame the newspapers, ma'am." And before I could get in a word, he said, "To the Tower it will be, and I will make sure you don't lose your head."

I grimaced, but laughed aloud at the grisly reference.

The Tower of London has seen a lot of misery and death. But there is a brighter side as well. Mr. Franklin showed me the baptismal font for the royal family and the horse armory. I saw the crowns in their gilded cages, the diamonds and jewels, including the famous ruby from India, I saw the scepters. I listened with rapt attention as Mr. Franklin pointed out the one that had belonged to murderous Henry VIII, the king who loved to behead his wives. I was impressed and told Mr. Franklin so.

"Well, I am glad of it," he said. "But, one day, we in America too will build an impressive civilization." I could not but agree.

To my great pleasure, Mr. James Albert Ukawsaw Gronniosaw visited me at the countess's home. He was part of Lady Huntingdon's evangelical assembly, pious men and women who believe in taking the Gospel to all in the kingdom of Great Britain, America and the islands of the seas.

"Truly, I cannot hide my pleasure, Miss Wheatley, to meet such a noble and talented member of my race," he said to me.

"The pleasure is mine, Mr. Gronniosaw," I replied.

"The countess tells me you do not possess a copy of my book, so it behooves me to present one to you." And, to my great delight, Mr. Gronniosaw pressed a copy into my hand.

"Believe me, Mr. Gronniosaw, when I tell you this is one of the best gifts I have ever received."

I know Mr. Gronniosaw's story well. The noble soul was born in Bornu in West Africa, but was kidnapped into slavery. In London, he was enslaved to a wealthy seaman, but later gained his freedom. The book tells of his kidnapping from his beloved family and homeland, the dreadful journey across the Atlantic Ocean chained in the hold of a vile slave ship and his ordeal in bondage.

Mr. Gronniosaw said he had come to take me to see the Changing of the Guard at Buckingham Palace, but, as it had started to rain intensely, it was best to stay inside. We conversed for hours, until the purple of twilight filled the room and the servants lit the lamps.

My time in London was full. Yet, sometimes, I felt like a specimen under a microscope. Some people expressed surprise at my good speech and formal grammar. They claimed that they did not know a Black person could speak so well and have such a command of the English language. Others asked me directly if it was I who wrote the poems. I grew weary of their prodding. Their questions disappointed me. There were several Black writers in England. Why did the White people display such suspicion about my talents? Did they not know of these writers living in their midst? I fear that even if a thousand Black geniuses in all the arts and sciences were to be paraded before these doubting Thomases, they would still cling to their beliefs because they *want* to.

For all its glitter, London is a damp, dark city. It rained incessantly, and there were whole days when it seemed a perpetual, cold twilight. The dampness crept into me, and there were entire days when I stayed in my room by the fire warming my bones. I began to cough unceasingly, and that was quieted only by a syrupy potion that Amelia made. I do not have a strong constitution. When I lived in Fouta Toro, I was strong and never ill. All that changed when I crossed the Atlantic Ocean that first time.

CHAPTER ELEVEN

Back to Boston

Toward the end of July, a summons came for me to leave London. My mistress had fallen gravely ill, and my master wrote to Nathaniel, asking him to send me home to nurse her. I would have wished to stay in London to see the publication of my book. But I could not. Moreover, London's damp had penetrated my bones, and my last days there were filled with a gloom that refused to lift, in spite of the accolades.

When duty calls you must obey. But this was more than duty and obedience. It was also gratitude and, dare I say, love. Susanna Wheatley had been my one true friend and supporter. She had rescued me from certain death as I lay weak, sick and cold on the dock that July morning in 1761. The captain had left me to die, but she bought me.

She gave me a decent life. She taught me to read, write and speak. She gave me my tongue. My master saw to it that I was used well and insisted that others in Boston recognize my talents, but my mistress got my poems published in New England's and Pennsylvania's leading newspapers. She made sure that my book would be published. Most of all, she became my mother when I would never see my own mother again. And I knew that my mistress not only took pity on me but had grown to love me. And I loved her in return.

So when the letter came from Boston, I packed my trunks. My master's ship, the *London Packet*, was still in England, and Nathaniel arranged my passage on it.

Lady Huntingdon urged me to stay in London. She had secured an audience for me with the king himself, George the Third. Imagine! Imagine what I could write Obour if I had met the king! I imagined telling my friend Scipio Moorehead, the celebrated African portrait painter. It made me giddy just to think about it. But not even royalty could prevent me from returning to Boston.

Nathanial visited me at Lady Huntingdon's.

"I am afraid Mother is dying, Phillis."

I shook my head vigorously and said, "Don't say so. Mistress is strong. She has many years left." But I said that more for my benefit than Nathaniel's.

"My mother loves Aunt Betty, and Aunt Betty is an excellent nurse; but without a doubt, Phillis, it is you whom my sick mother wants by her side."

"I would prefer it, too."

"Phillis, here you can have your freedom. If you stayed in England, you would be a free woman."

It was an idea that had filled my every hour since my arrival in London, especially after I met Granville Sharp. I had friends in London who would help me with the legal work necessary to gain my freedom, and they would assist me in establishing myself here. But I knew I would return to America. My close friends were there, and I was bound, in part by love, to my mistress.

I did not respond to Nathaniel's words, but studied my palms. I knew not what he read of my silence, but he said, "I have written to my father that, if you ever returned to Boston, he should set you free."

My final evening was spent with a small group of London's literati. We read poetry and discussed diverse matters. Just when I thought I would leave London with all pleasant memories, a man stood up and pointed his finger at me. "Madam, you claim to be the authoress of these verses. I have lived in the West Indies, and I have never seen or heard of a

Negro creating literature. Madam, I believe you are an impostor."

My blood boiled. I wanted to seize him by the collar and throttle him. I jumped to my feet, but the Earl of Dartmouth was faster than I. He placed himself between the offender and myself.

"Sir, I think you had better leave."

Lady Huntingdon clapped her hands, and Winston, a manservant, emerged from the shadows. "Winston, please escort Mr. Blaines."

But there was no need. Mr. Blaines had already gathered his coat and was making his way toward the door. But my rage did not leave with him.

The next day, Benjamin Franklin, James Gronniosaw, Brook Watson and Nathaniel accompanied me to the Port of London. I expressed my sincere thanks to all of them and boarded the *London Packet*. On board, I confined myself to my cabin, on my knees. "Lord, let my mistress live. Rescue her from the jaws of death. Restore her to health. And if she is to die, my Lord, let me see her alive before she departs this world. Send your Son to comfort her. Amen." Not even the sighting of whales off Nova Scotia could budge me from my supplications.

I arrived in Boston in early September and took full charge of my mistress. Aunt Betty had grown more arthritic; climbing up and down the stairs was painful and difficult for her. My mistress was indeed gravely ill. She had consumption. She coughed all night and all day, and a harsh, grating sound came from her chest. She had lost a lot of weight because she vomited up most of what she ate. I nursed her, read to her, fussed over her and prayed with and for her. I could not hide my feelings and cried freely. At such times she would squeeze my hand and say, "Dear girl, I will be all right. You will be, too. Have faith."

I redoubled my prayers and started a fast, but my weight loss was noticeable.

"You are much too slim to be without food. No more fasting," my mistress commanded. "Do not do that on my account. God wants us to eat."

I had to smile in spite of my grief. My mistress was ever so practical.

In the midst of my ministrations, my life changed once more. Early one afternoon, after I had given my mistress dosages of a syrupy and bitter potion the doctor had mandated, my master called me to the drawing room. Sitting with him was John Wainscoat, the family lawyer. I wondered if my master wanted me to read poetry for them.

"Phillis, Mr. Wainscoat is here to draw up your manumission papers."

"Sir?"

"I am granting you your freedom."

My heart turned inside my chest. I was to be liberated. Was this Nathaniel's doing? Tears spilled down my face. I dared not speak.

During my time in England, several and various newspapers published articles about my poetry, my "prodigious" talent, and lamented the fact that I was a slave. They called the Americans hypocrites for wanting freedom from Britain but withholding it from their enslaved Africans. "Miss Wheatley is a good example of the genius held in captive by American slavery," one newspaper pronounced. I had sailed back to America with copies of these papers. I did not show them to my master or mistress, but I am sure Nathaniel sent copies to them. Our colonial newspapers also reprint much of what appears in the London papers.

Once I had agreed to return to look after my mistress, the Wheatleys knew they were in my debt. I had made with them a silent and unwritten contract: If I returned to America, the Wheatleys would grant me my freedom.

Though I had been treated more like a favored servant than a slave, the fact remained that John and Susanna Wheatley owned me and, if they were to die, their children would inherit me. To be free. To be free. What did that really mean? My master was about to let me know the answer.

I sank to my knees in gratitude and kissed my master's hands.

"Rise, my child. You have earned the right to be free. God knows our colonies are clamoring for their freedom from Britain. How can we nurture a more poisonous form of slavery?" My master, soon to be my former master, spoke these latter words almost to himself.

"Miss Phillis." The voice of Mr. Wainscoat brought me back to the matter at hand. "The papers are drawn up. All you have to do is sign this certificate of manumission."

And so it was that I was granted my freedom. I signed my American name, Phillis Wheatley, to the certificate, but it was Penda Wane who had been freed. Or had she?

My mother was dead and, likely, my father, little

Chierno and the baby, too. What had happened to Amadi? I thought of my capture, kidnapping and the horrific journey on the slave ship. It had broken my health. To this day, my lungs are weak and I suffer from asthma. Nathaniel once told me that if I could forget these horrors, my asthma would go away. I believed him, but how could I forget such an ordeal?

However, in order to show my gratitude, I told my master that I would remain and look after my mistress. He had expected that, though he nodded mournfully. To experience my new state, when my mistress slept in the afternoon, I left her in the care of Aunt Betty and Clara and wandered to the bank of the river. I walked and walked and walked, and I did not feel the cold until I had to face the future: How would I look after myself once I left the Wheatleys?

CHAPTER TWELVE

My Books Arrive

The countess sent me my books! They came through Newport in November. The harbor master sent me a letter saying that the books were on their way, and they were delivered in Boston two days later. My master instructed Prince to fetch the cargo, but I jumped in the coach beside him. I was too excited to wait. Fifteen crates of books! I held one of the slim volumes in my hands, and my heart fluttered. My book. *Poems on Various Subjects, Religious and Moral*. An engraving of my profile on the cover. The painting was commissioned by the countess from my friend, Scipio Moorehead. I turned to the first page and read the dedication: "To the Right Honourable the Countess of Huntingdon." It was my mistress's idea that I dedicate the book to the countess.

I felt the sun coursing through my veins, through my blood.

"Phillis, God bless you. The whole race blesses you." Prince's voice broke my reverie.

His face was filled with the light of his smile. Prince had been my friend from the day I walked into the Wheatley house, a trembling, sick and frightened girl. As I grew stronger, he showed me around Boston. He showed me the meadows where he picked dandelion greens for our cook. He withstood my mistress's anger when she caught him talking to me. He said nothing when she raged at him after I sat with him at the front of the coach. *The whole race blesses you.* My book was not only for me but for Prince, Aunt Betty and Clara — and for the future.

I sent a crate of books to Obour Tanner in Providence with instructions on how to distribute them. Two crates had remained in Newport for sale there. I sent books to Concord, New Haven, Philadelphia and New York. My mistress, though ill, with my assistance wrote letters to her friends, relatives and acquaintances, urging them to buy my book. My former master instructed me to send a crate each to two merchant friends, one in Halifax, Nova Scotia, and the other in Kingston, Jamaica.

But the crate from Jamaica was returned: the government there had banned my book. The authorities said that it was subversive, that Blacks held there in slavery might rebel if they learned that one of their race had written a book!

One evening, after returning from my walk, I saw Prince with the carriage outside the Wheatley house. I gave him a warm hello. He handed me a letter.

Dear Miss Wheatley, let me be the first (though I am sure I'm not) to congratulate you on the publication of your book. I have bought a copy and have read it more than three times.

As an African myself, I take great pride in knowing that one of our race has uplifted the race in so high a manner.

When I am in Boston, may I have the pleasure of calling on you?

I look forward to your reply.

Your humble servant,
John Peters

This could only be *the* John Peters, the free Black man who owned a grocery store in Boston and was studying law with the solicitor John Deerhouse. I immediately wrote back, thanking Mr. Peters for his support and telling him his visit would please me greatly.

But another letter touched my heart even more. It came from a fellow Black poet, Jupiter Hammon of Long Island. He congratulated me, thanked me for my "gifts and talents" and "for uplifting the African race." He enclosed a poem he had written in my honor.

Numerous invitations came for me. I gave more readings in the drawing rooms of Boston than ever before. Newspapers across the land reviewed my book favorably. "Brilliant verses from a Negro girl." "A credit to American society and learning." There was only one critical review, from the pen of a man who owned many slaves yet was quickly gaining a reputation as a revolutionary: Thomas Jefferson. Mr. Jefferson had nothing good to say about my poems. But let him be. It was not for me to convince him of my worth.

In the month that followed my receipt of the books, I received a letter from the countess. The booksellers of London had sold all my books and had undertaken a second printing! Books were also sold in Dublin and Belfast, in Glasgow and Edinburgh. The countess said that the London papers had reviewed my book favorably. In her letter, she enclosed a money order (of fifty pounds!) and a review from the famous French philosopher Monsieur Voltaire, who said that I wrote "good verses."

In spite of my mistress's illness, my life was sweet. Men doffed their hats to me in the streets. Black people, both slave and free, ran to shake my hand. Prince found the most delicious greens for Aunt Betty to cook for me. "So you can be strong," he said to me. And for those months, my asthma disappeared completely.

As it turned out, my books arrived just in time. A few weeks later came the Boston Tea Party. The colonists had refused to let ships laden with "British" tea unload. They were incensed that they had to pay a duty on the tea and that the British East India Company had a monopoly and could run the colonial merchants out of business. They felt that Governor Hutchinson, one of my examiners, had insulted them, had no regard for them and was a traitor.

So on the evening of 16 December 1773, about forty men dressed as Mohawk Indians boarded the ships, smashed open the cases of tea and dumped it in the harbor. The governor and colonial officials were furious, and the incident was raised in Parliament. Britain decided to close the port. Angry mobs responded by storming Governor Hutchinson's house, breaking his furniture and destroying his papers. As no ships could enter or leave the port of Boston, John Wheatley's imports from the West Indies and Britain could not get in, and his exports could not leave either. But my books were safe. Thank God.

By the new year, it appeared that Susanna Wheatley would recover. She was able to take more food. Her skin glowed, and she breathed more easily. But it was all a deception. At the beginning of March, she took a turn for the worse. On the fourteenth day of the month, I bathed her, fed her soup, read the scriptures and prayed with her. After prayers, she said, "I'm going, Phillis. I feel my angel calling me. My body cannot live much longer."

"Nonsense, Madam. You will be here for many more years."

But fear gripped me as I said those empty words.

I smoothed her pillow and held her hand. She slept, her breathing even and her face peaceful. I must have fallen asleep, and I woke up with a start. I felt cold. The room was chilly. Alarmed, I looked at my mistress. She opened her eyes ever so slightly.

"Phillis, call my dear husband and the entire household." I could not hold back my tears. "Dear girl, don't cry. Do as I ask."

I yelled at Prince to get Reverend Cooper from next door, and we all gathered around. My mistress held my master's hand and mine. Reverend Cooper prayed amid our weeping. He said that "Zion needs Susanna Wheatley more than Earth."

My mistress spoke my name in a whisper.

"Yes, ma'am."

"When I am gone, write no verses for me. No funeral songs, no elegies. I want to be remembered as a humble soul. Promise me this."

But I could not speak for the lump in my throat.

"Promise," she said again, as she squeezed my hand.

"Yes, ma'am, yes."

Her final words were "Serve the Lord. Serve the Lord." And then she died.

We buried her in the South End Church cemetery. All of Boston was at the funeral. Everyone had loved her. Her daughter, Mary, wailed beyond comfort. Nothing her husband did could console her. Her cries pierced my heart, and I patted her shoulder. Mary turned and said, "Poor us, Phillis, poor us. What shall we do now that Mother is gone? Phillis, you cannot know what it is to lose a mother."

A loud roar filled my head. *You cannot know what it is to lose a mother*? Surely Mary could not have been thinking clearly. Surely grief must have dented her mind. I not know what it is to lose a mother? I had lost two mothers. Grief had made Mary cruel.

After the funeral I repaired to my room, bolted the door and told myself I'd stay there forever. But after just a few hours, I had an asthma attack. My lungs felt as if they were squeezed by iron hands, and for the next three days it appeared that I would join my mistress in Zion.

Aunt Betty nursed me back to life, but I did not want to live. "Leave me alone. I want to die, too." Those words sounded so familiar. And then I remembered. I had said them over and over to the woman in green on the slave ship. She had told me that I could not die, that the ancestors would not allow me to die. I watched Aunt Betty's lips and, as if in a dream, I heard her say the same thing. But I was beyond caring. She who had given me my life back had left me.

Susanna Wheatley's death filled me with a loneliness that weighed on me like a giant stone. Loneliness was not new. It had been a part of me since I was dragged from Africa. But, over time, it had subsided and lodged itself in a small place inside me. Now it rose and threatened to crush me. I wished it would. I wanted to compose an elegy for my mistress, despite her admonitions, but the words refused to come. I, who had written elegies for many of Boston's dead, was now struck mute on the passing of my mistress, the woman who gave me my voice.

CHAPTER THIRTEEN

Revolution

Boston was all aflame. British soldiers had waged a pitched battle with a bunch of revolutionary hotheads. Young Bostonians had thrown snowballs at the soldiers, who then fired into the crowd, killing five men. The first to die was Crispus Attucks, a man of mixed African and Indian ancestry. He became the first martyr of the Revolution. People called the shootings a massacre. I could hear the roar of the guns and the answering roar of the crowd. The Revolution had begun.

In September 1774, Boston came under British occupation. Many, including my master and I, fled the city. We lodged in Providence in the house of my master's daughter, Mary. Amid the gloom was one bright spark — Obour Tanner.

"When the war ends — and we will have war for sure — if the Americans win, they will free their slaves. They talk too much about freedom for it not to be freedom for everyone!" Obour said.

"Britain could win," I replied, "and if she does, I believe our freedom will be more secure."

Obour looked at me as if my words were treasonous. "America will win!" she said excitedly.

"I hope so, because I chose to come back to America. I have cast my lot with her."

My former master and I missed Boston. As well, he was worried about his house. "Anything could happen," he said. I think he was worried that Prince and Rufus, and even Clara and Aunt Betty, left by themselves, might run off. So we returned to Boston.

All talk was about fighting Britain. The British army left Boston in 1775, and an army of Patriots, as the Americans called themselves, occupied the city. George Washington, a southern planter who owned more than two hundred slaves, was the head of the American army. Mr. Washington had fought in the Seven Years War against the French and the Indians. In April 1775, on Lexington Green, just a few miles outside of Boston, British troops traded fire with a Patriot militia. The war had begun.

John Wheatley's world was falling apart. He had built his wealth on trade within the British Empire. The mother country had been good to him, and he was deeply loyal. I thought of the countess, my master and mistress and even Governor Hutchinson. Loyalists all, and each in their way responsible for who I had become. But, according to the Patriots, these people were *enemies* of America! And yet, I had written poems about the unfairness of the Stamp Act and other injustices endured by the colonists. When the Earl of Dartmouth arrived as the secretary of the colonies, I heralded him in verse and advised that he act fairly with us. Britain was the great mother lion, and we looked to her for protection. We, the colonies, were the cubs of the great lioness. But the lioness acted treacherously toward her cubs. When the cubs became strong, they challenged the mother. With each victory, their fear of her dissipated.

I loved Britain. But I understood the heart of the colonists, the striving to be free from tyranny and servitude. Words of the Declaration of Independence gave me hope. "We hold these truths to be self-evident, that all men are created equal." And that is why I threw in my lot with the Patriots.

Yet it was not blind support. George Washington had not emancipated his slaves, even as he shouted that Britain held America in chains. And did Thomas Jefferson think of the Black men he owned when he wrote, "All men are created equal"? Some slaveholders, seeing the contradiction, released their human chattel. I heard the talk in church; I read it in the papers. And my Black brethren, too, challenged their owners and clamored for their freedom. Twice that year the Sons of Africa presented petitions to the Massachusetts Assembly, demanding a general emancipation for all Africans in bondage in the colony. I felt it in my bones — freedom would come.

Yet the Patriots lost several key battles, and there were strict rationings. Soldiers visited Boston homes and took whatever food and supplies they found. When they found the kitchens empty, they ransacked the cellars. Two soldiers came to the Wheatley home, but when they discovered who I was, they engaged me in a discussion about literature and left without searching the house. I breathed a sigh of relief, for I had a whole side of roasted lamb hidden in the pantry.

We could not have any discussion about the war. The Patriots called dissenting opinion "unpatriotic," and whoever uttered it was tarred and feathered or even killed. War raged around me, and another raged in my heart. I grieved as many of my friends, people who had supported my poetry, left for England, never to return. Yet I knew I could not go with them. John Wheatley had given me my freedom. That meant I had to choose my place in this new order.

Aunt Betty, Prince, Clara and Rufus joined the British Loyalist forces. The British promised freedom to any slaves who deserted their owners and joined them. The Patriot Army made no such promise. Thousands of enslaved Africans fled to the Loyalist Army. Still, I remained safely in the Wheatley house and looked after my former master.

George Washington had established the army headquarters in Cambridge, a few miles outside of Boston. A daring idea formed in my mind. I wrote to General Washington, enclosing a poem in his honor: "To His Excellency, General Washington."

Proceed great chief, with virtue on thy side,
Thy ev'ry action let the goddess guide.
A crown, a mansion, and a throne that shine,
With gold unfading, WASHINGTON! be thine.

He wrote back and invited me to visit him at his camp.

The general received me with warmth and hospitality. He praised my poetry, and I praised his courage and what he was doing for America. What I saw in his camp warmed my heart. Free Black men had joined the Patriots' army, and I saw them in General Washington's camp in uniform, some even holding rifles and bayonets. Black men defending the cause of the Patriots and, it is hoped, the cause of freedom. It had been argued that Africans do not make good soldiers, but here they were in the camp, even if most were laborers. And General Washington told me that the African soldiers were courageous fighters.

I returned to Boston more convinced that I must support the Patriots and use my energies and talents to battle for freedom. With this conviction, my loneliness began to lift.

CHAPTER FOURTEEN

John Peters

It was while visiting Scipio Moorehead that I finally met John Peters. Scipio had painted the likeness of dozens of New England's most prominent citizens. After Scipio painted the profile that graced my book, he wrote to say that he wanted to paint my full portrait. After some delay, to Mr. Moorehead's I went. I dressed in a red damask gown with a low-cut bodice. Susanna Wheatley would have said that too much of my bosom showed. But I was my own woman now. Nor did I cover my hair, but left it free. My short locks curled on my head, as they had in Fouta, and I liked the effect.

When I arrived at Scipio's, *he* was there. John Peters. "You must be the celebrated Miss Wheatley," he said, extending his hand. His shake was firm. I liked that. "John Peters at your service," he said.

I liked his voice. Well modulated and strong. His complexion was as dark as mine. He looked like the men of my country and was as tall as my father.

Hours later, when Scipio showed me the portrait, I gasped. Was that me? This girl with such determination in her eyes? The portrait was exquisite.

John Peters looked at the painting for a long time before he said, "This is a masterpiece."

By the time Scipio had finished my portrait, darkness had fallen. Scipio insisted that I stay for supper, but I declined due to the lateness of the hour. John Peters offered to walk me home. I was grateful for that and happy for his company. I liked his quiet but purposeful presence.

And that was the beginning. Oftentimes, when Mr. Peters called on me, we would go walking. I told John what I had previously told only to Obour, of the loss of my family and country and the awful journey into slavery. I told him these sorrows one fine summer afternoon, as we strolled through the Common. He listened keenly, and his tears fell. "Our people have suffered so much, Phillis, but we must trust in the Almighty to see us through."

John was born in Massachusetts, his parents in New York, but he believed that his grandparents came from Africa. I told him that they must have come from Fouta because he looked so much like the men of my country. When I said that, he took my hand. I did not take it away. A sweet silence descended on us, and we walked in its embrace.

It was Christmas 1777 when John asked me to marry him. A perfect day to say yes to a new life. And that was my answer: yes.

Mr. Wheatley, my former master, was gravely ill, and I could not in good conscience leave him to marry John. I celebrated Christmas with John, Scipio and John Wheatley at the Wheatley residence. How I missed Aunt Betty and Prince!

After John and Scipio left, my former master said, "John is reaching too much ahead of himself."

"What do you mean, sir?"

"He ought to be content with his station in life. Why does he want to be a lawyer?"

I was dumbfounded. Finally, I found my voice. "Sir, you saw to it that I received an education, and you always told me to believe in myself. I do not understand your feelings about John."

"Your mistress ... and later myself ... saw that you

had a fine mind. At first, we could not believe it because we were not used to ..."

"Don't say it!" I screamed at him.

"It was but an experiment, Phillis, if a successful one. Your mistress would think that you are too good for him."

For the first time in the seventeen years that I had lived with John Wheatley, we quarreled. I retired to my room with a migraine.

In the new year, Mr. Wheatley became sicker and sicker, and on 3 March he met his maker, almost four years precisely after his wife and my former mistress had passed away. John Wheatley never completely recovered from the death of his wife. He had also lost his children, but in a different way. Nathaniel remained in England and married into a successful merchant family. Mary had married Reverend Lathrope and lived in Providence. And all the slaves had joined the Loyalists. The war made him insecure and vulnerable. He had seen his beloved Boston and Massachusetts, which used to be a bedrock of stability, sink into chaos, and he lost his grounding. He did not wish to be a part of the new order. But I had less sympathy for him than I used to have, since that night of our quarrel.

A few days after John Wheatley's death, his lawyer, Mr. Wainscoat, came to the house. Mary and her husband, two brothers of my former master, and a lawyer representing Nathaniel gathered in the Wheatley home to hear the will read. Mr. Wheatley left his business, his ship, the house and money to Nathaniel. Mary he also remembered.

He left nothing to me. Not one penny, not even a plate. This man, who freely had taken my labor for all those years, left me not even a stale biscuit. Did he feel that he had given me enough by helping me to become a published and celebrated poet? By giving me my freedom? I had hoped for something from my former master to acknowledge all I had done for him. But that was not to be. Like the rest of the world, I must march on.

With John Wheatley's death, I was free to marry John Peters. I wrote to Obour Tanner.

12 March 1778
Boston
Dear Obour:

My friend, John Peters, whom I wrote you about, has asked me to marry him, and I have agreed. We will be married on 2 April. It would be my

147

*sincere pleasure if you would stand as my witness.
I will pay for your passage from Providence. May
you remain in good health and under God's
guidance.*

*Your friend,
Phillis*

Obour came, and the wedding took place at
John's house on Queen Street. Scipio Moorehead
shook my hand and John's and embraced us both.
Many members of Boston's free Black community
came, as John was well known and I likewise.

I moved out of the Wheatley home, not without
difficulty. I had come to life in that place. I had
been shown love and kindness by everyone within.
I would not forget that. I stood by my window for
the last time and looked at the scene below. So
many times I had sat at my desk, poetry flowing
from my mind. Now I saw soldiers marching. The
beginning of a new order.

John came by with a coach to fetch my things. I
rode with him in silence. It seemed a thousand
years since I had come to Massachusetts, and a
thousand thoughts crowded my mind. The end of
an old life; the beginning of a new one. I thought

of the new poems I was writing. Poems about freedom, about slavery, about the Revolution. And about my feelings for John. I was now a married woman. Mrs. Phillis Peters. It sounded good in my heart and made me smile.

Many of my friends and members of the Wheatleys' extended family were concerned about my marrying John. They felt that, having been pampered and shielded from hard work, I ought not to enter a more difficult life. True, I was more used to handling a pen than a brush or broom, but I was my own woman now and had to make my life. Though he was not as wealthy as my former master, John was financially secure. His house, our house, was in one of Boston's best neighborhoods, with such prominent neighbors as the great political leaders Josiah Quincy and John Adams. John had also procured for me two servants, one of my own race.

"Phillis, I have been thinking."

"About?"

"Do you have plans for a second book?"

I laughed aloud.

"Did I say something wrong?"

"No, not at all. I was thinking about the new

poems I am composing," I said. "You read my mind."

"Good, then we must get them published."

That he had read my mind made me hopeful for my life with him. I would like to have children. I would name a daughter Penda, or Susanna after my mistress. I felt the power surging in my mind. A thousand words crowded my head. My fingers itched. So many poems to write. On the slave ship, the woman in green had told me that I had survived for a reason. That I could not die. Did I live so I could become "the first Black person in America to publish a book," as the newspapers described me? Did I live only to prove that the African had a fine mind? That the African could think and write?

John's presence was warm and solid. I leaned my head on his shoulder. A warm breeze from the east caressed us as we embarked on our journey. My heart was filled with gladness. The coach stopped in front of the house where I was to begin my new life as Phillis Peters. John jumped down and stretched his hand to me. "Come, Phillis," he said. And I joined my hand with his and stepped from the coach.

An Hymn to the Evening

Soon as the sun forsook the eastern main
The pealing thunder shook the heav'nly plain;
Majestic grandeur! From the zephyr's wing,
Exhales the incense of the blooming spring.
Soft purl the streams, the birds renew their notes,
And through the air their mingled music floats.
Through all the heav'ns what beauteous dies are spread!
But the west glories in the deepest red:
So may our breasts with ev'ry virtue glow,
The living temples of our God below!...

Phillis Peters, formerly Phillis Wheatley

Boston, April 1778

Epilogue

During the early years of her marriage, Phillis produced another manuscript of poetry. As with her first book, however, no American publisher was willing to print it. Most of the poems in this second manuscript have disappeared over time.

The Revolution ended in 1783. Although it brought about the independence of the American colonies from Britain, it did not end slavery or bring equal rights for free Black citizens. In supporting the Revolution, Phillis had envisioned a multiracial society in which everyone had the same rights and freedoms, but this was not to be. The post-Revolutionary period had no place for a Black woman who was intelligent, talented and educated.

Phillis and John Peters had three children, all of whom died in infancy. In 1784 at around thirty-one years old, Phillis died in childbirth; the child also died. Phillis Wheatley Peters was mourned by her husband and friends, yet she had launched a poetic tradition that thousands would follow.